AXEL

THE CHAOS DEMONS MC

NICOLA JANE

AXEL

The Chaos Demons MC

By
Nicola Jane

This book is a work of fiction. The names, characters, places, and incidents are all products of the author's imagination and are not to be construed as real. Any similarities are entirely coincidental.

AXEL Copyright © 2023 by Nicola Jane. All rights are reserved. No part of this

book may be used or reproduced in any manner without written permission from the author,

except in the case of brief quotations used in articles or reviews. For information, contact Nicola Jane.

Cover Designer: Wingfield Designs

Editor: Rebecca Vazquez, Dark Syde Books

Proofreader: Jackie Ziegler, Dark Syde Books

Formatting: Nicola Miller

Formatting: V.R Formatting

Spelling Note

Please note, this author resides in the United Kingdom and is using British English. Therefore, some words may be viewed as incorrect or spelled incorrectly, however, they are not.

Trigger warning

This book contains triggers for violence, explicit scenes, and some dirty talking bikers. If any of this offends you, put your concerns in writing to Axel, he'll get back to you . . . maybe.

Acknowledgments

Thank you to all my wonderful readers—you rock!

Playlist:

Hurricane - Luke Combs
What Now - Rihanna
Demons - Imagine Dragons
Every Breath You Take - The Police
greedy - Tate McRae
Just a Fool - Christina Aguilera ft. Blake Shelton
Mercy - Brett Young
Love Is Blind - Nate Smith
How You Remind Me - Nickelback
breathin - Ariana Grande
What Now - Rihanna
Someday - Nickelback
Stay - Rihanna ft. Mikky Ekko
Still into You - Paramore

CHAPTER 1

LEXI

I clink glasses with Verity. "Congratulations, and although we'll be so sad to see you leave, you totally deserve this break in your career."

I smile, sipping my glass of cheap fizz. "It's not forever."

"And you won't get lonely. My sister is a total blast," Ben adds.

I smile gratefully. He arranged for his sister and her friends to take me under their wings when I arrive in Manchester tomorrow. I've lived my entire life here in Nottingham, but I've finally had the break I've been wanting. The top dogs in Manchester requested me personally. *Me!* My sergeant, Grace, told me she was singing my praises when they called to ask about me, but I'd like to think they decided on me because of my hard work on the police force over the last four years.

When I first joined up, I made it no secret I wanted to work for a bigger force. London, Manchester, anywhere with a big city. The thought of busy crowds and bustling night life appealed to me, and although London is the dream, this is certainly a step in the right direction. "It won't be long before we're calling you 'ma'am'," adds Verity with a laugh.

I roll my eyes. "I think I'll need a few more years behind me before that happens."

I get home an hour later and let myself into the three-bed, semi-detached house I share with my dad.

I find Dad in the kitchen cooking, and I smile when I peer into the pan he's stirring and see he's making my favourite, leek and potato soup. I give him a kiss on the cheek. "When you said you were going for a drink after work, I assumed you'd be out late," he says, checking his watch. "Eight o'clock is a new record for you."

"I've still got to pack," I remind him. It's all been very last minute, with the call to request my transfer being just a few days ago.

He continues to stir, not moving his eyes from the soup, and asks, "You're sure about this, right, Lex?"

I get two bowls from the cupboard and place them on the side. "We've been over this."

"It just seems so rushed. And Manchester is so . . . big."

I grin. "I'm a big girl, Dad. I can handle it."

He pours soup into the bowls, and I carry them to the table, where he joins me. "What if you get lost?"

"What if I don't?" I taste the soup and close my eyes in pure bliss. He's the best home cook ever.

"I have enough sleepless nights as it is and you're here. I don't know how I'll cope when you're there."

I take pity on him and give his hand a sympathetic squeeze. "I'll call you after every shift, or at least send a text. I'm good at my job, and there'll be the same crime there, just more of it. And I stand more of a chance cli—"

"Climbing the ranks," he cuts in, laughing. "I know, I know, you keep telling me. But what's wrong with staying as you are?"

I place my spoon down and stare him in the eye. "What's really going on, Dad?"

He takes a minute before sighing. "What if you see her?"

This time, I take both his hands in my own. "What are the chances of that happening? It's a huge place, and even if I did, she wouldn't recognise me now." He nods, but his expression tells me he's still worrying I might bump into my mother. The woman who abandoned us sixteen years ago, leaving Dad to raise me singlehandedly. "Anyway, we don't even know if she's still in Manchester. We don't even know if she's still alive. And I can't spend my entire life here, with you, just so you can protect me from her."

I've spent years wondering who she is now, if she's got a new family, and wondering why she never came to find me. But since joining the force, it's taken my focus from her, and I wouldn't want to see her these days, even if she called. I've got my Dad, and that's all I need, all I've ever needed.

He gives his shoulders a shake and releases a breath. "You're right, I'm sorry. I shouldn't be talking like this. This is an exciting opportunity for you, and I really am happy. I'm just gonna miss you so much."

AXEL

I drop my cigarette and crush it under my heavy boot while releasing the smoke from my lungs. I push off the wall and cross the street, heading towards The Zen Den, a massage parlour owned and ran by my club, The Chaos Demons.

Chas is on the front desk, and she glances up as I enter and plasters a huge, forced smile on her face. "Pres," she greets, coming around the desk to kiss me on the cheek. "What brings you here so early?"

"You look nervous, Chas," I state, stepping around her and parting the tacky door beads to peer into the back room.

Three girls are lounging around in underwear. They all

look strung out, not one of them bothering to look up as I enter. Chas is right behind me, clapping her hands to get their attention. "Look lively, ladies," she snaps.

"What are they on?" I ask.

"Axel, I don't know what they take before they turn up here."

"Get them out of here," I snap, stepping farther into the room.

"But they're needed. It's Thursday night, and we always get busy on a Thursday."

"Did I stutter?" I growl, moving through the room to the next.

I stand in the doorway to the kitchenette and take in the mess. Dishes are stacked up with old food rotting away. There're empty vodka bottles carelessly discarded. It's a tiny space, but one the punters have to go through to get to the stairs. I groan before swiping at the stacked dishes so they topple, smashing against the wall.

Chas flinches before turning back to the lifeless girls. "Someone clean this shit up. Now!"

"How many girls have you got up there tonight?" I ask, turning to face her.

"Six."

"Are they all strung out on some shit too?"

"Maybe, I don't know."

I pinch the bridge of my nose. "You're in charge," I snap. "You should know."

Grizz, my Vice President, steps into the room and takes in the state of the girls. He arches a brow then looks in my direction. "Thought you said meet at nine?" he asks, checking his watch.

"I got here early."

"I see the clean-up's begun," he adds, smirking at the broken plates.

We're interrupted when a man in his late sixties comes down the stairs followed by one of our girls who's still naked. She's staggering like she's drunk, and her hair hangs limp in her face. Bruises cover her sagging tits, and there's a string of red bruises around her neck which look to be love bites. I glare at Grizz with wide 'what the fuck' eyes, and he shrugs.

"You need me to handle these thugs, Chas?" the man asks, his voice croaky from too much smoking.

"No, thanks, Dave, you get on your way, and we'll see you tomorrow as usual," she replies, patting him on the shoulder and leading him out.

"You won't see him tomorrow. This place is closed for re-staffing," I snap.

She swings her head back around to glare at me. "What?"

"I didn't fucking stutter that time, Chas. Get everyone down here. I need to see the state of the others."

———

Half an hour later, I'm back in the clubhouse and calling church. I don't like anything I've seen in the last twenty-four hours, and my men need to know things are going to change.

I wait for them to settle before slamming the gavel on the old oak table to get their attention.

"What kind of fucking shitshow are we running here?" I ask, and before anyone can give me some smart answer that'll just piss me off further, I add, "Cos so far, I don't like anything I've seen. I got bookies giving out credit. Fucking credit to gamblers!" I yell. "I got whores so fucking high on drugs, they're not capable of walking let alone sucking cock. No wonder we're not making money."

"Pres." We all turn to stare at Cash, and he suddenly looks unsure of what he was about to say. But I nod, pushing him to continue. "With all due respect, you and Grizz have been gone a long time, and we did the best we could, but with Ice in charge, it was bound to be a fuck-up."

I take a steadying breath. He's right, Ice is a complete fuck-up, but there wasn't shit I could do about it while I was in prison. Ice was the VP to my father, Tank, who had been battling cancer for the last year. He lost his battle just a few months ago, leaving Ice to continue in my absence.

"There are enough men in this club to run some businesses," I snap. "It doesn't just fall on Ice."

The door opens and Ice strolls in. I arch a brow and fold my arms over my chest, waiting to hear his excuse this time. It's the third time he's showed up late this week, and in my eyes, that's a show of disrespect. "Nice of you to join us," I snap.

He gives an easy grin. "I was balls deep in Foxy."

I give Grizz another 'what the fuck' glare, and again, he shrugs, shaking his head. "Sit the fuck down," I order, and he does, not looking bothered by my tone. "Who's supplying the girls at Zen?" I ask.

"That would be Nick Matthews," says Ice.

I frown. "Why does his name ring a bell?"

"It should, he's big time these days. He runs half the streets around here with his drugs."

"Get me a sample," I say. "I wanna know what's in the shit he's pushing to my girls."

"And what do you plan on doing when you find out?" asks Ice with a smirk.

"I plan on taking over."

CHAPTER 2

LEXI

The fully furnished flat I managed to rent is perfect. It's a ten-minute drive from the police station and well within my price budget. After I sign for the keys, the letting agent leaves, and the first thing I do is explore.

The flat is one of five in an old, converted Victorian-style house. My flat consists of one bedroom, a kitchen, and a small living room. It's perfect for me until I find my feet here.

I don't have time to unpack properly as I have a meeting with my new sergeant to discuss shift patterns and maybe meet who I'll be partnered up with. So, I shower and dress in jeans and a shirt then head out, deciding to walk to the station to get to know the area a little better.

I'm rounding the corner when I hear the rumble of motorbikes. It's so loud, I wince, and as they crawl past, the biker at the front turns his head to look at me. I don't catch a glimpse of his face as his helmet has the visor down, but he stares right until he gets to the end of my street before turning right and disappearing out of view. It brings back memories of my childhood, before Dad rescued me, and I shudder.

The station is busy. Way busier than my old station in Nottingham. I go to the desk and introduce myself, telling the officer I'm there for a meeting. I'm let in through the side door and led up the stairs to the offices, where a woman in a suit greets me in the corridor. "Alexia?" I nod, and she holds out her hand, which I shake. "Pleased to finally meet you. I'm Chief Superintendent Karen Taylor." She shows me into a board-style room with a large table and points to a seat. I lower into it, and she sits opposite me.

"I hope you don't mind, some of my colleagues will be joining us shortly."

"Oh. Am I interviewing?" I ask, suddenly feeling nervous. "I was told I didn't need to interview, that they wanted me on merit, so I'm not properly prepared."

"No. They'll be bringing you up to speed on the position we're offering."

I frown. "I thought that was all sorted. Isn't it a straight transfer for six months?"

She hesitates, then she smiles past me to two men who enter the room and seat themselves near the head of the table. I stand and shake hands as Karen introduces them as Commander Ian Smithe and Assistant Commissioner Alan Collinson. I suddenly feel out of my depth, unsure why these men from the top of the chain need to speak to me about a police constable role.

We all sit down, and Smithe opens a blue paper file. I see my picture clipped to the top. "Alexia Cooper," he begins. "Daughter of Gary Cooper, a lorry driver from Nottingham and Deborah Stevens, a drug addict from Manchester."

"I don't understand what's happening," I say, and my voice comes out much quieter than I want it to.

"You once lived here in Manchester?" asks Collinson.

"When I was a lot younger. I left when I was seven."

"And you've lived in Nottingham since?" I nod. "Do you have any contact with your mother?"

"No."

"When was the last time you saw her?" Smithe asks.

I glance at Karen, who looks uncomfortable. "Am I missing something?" I ask. "Because I thought I came here for a role as a police officer?"

"The last time?" Smithe repeats.

I sigh. "When I left sixteen years ago."

"Do you think you'd recognise her again if you saw her in the street?"

I shrug. "I have no idea."

He slides a picture from the file towards me, and I stare at it. My heart stutters at the sight of my mother. Her face is exactly how I remember it, just older and more tired. I slide it away. "What is this about?"

"What we're about to tell you stays in this room," says Smithe, "but you're not here for a standard policing role."

AXEL

Grizz props his feet up on my desk and leans back in the chair. "You think the men are happy with the new roles?" he asks.

I shrug. I couldn't give a shit. I'm running the club my way. "They have two choices—deal with it or fuck off."

"Come on, Ax, you don't mean that. Some of these guys have been loyal to your dad. They're a good bunch, they just need some clear guidance."

"And Ice?" I ask, arching a brow.

He grins. "Well, Ice is completely pissed about his demotion, but he's disguising it well." We both laugh, knowing Ice is taking it pretty hard he's no longer VP. "He's definitely one I wouldn't mind seeing the back of."

Grizz slides his feet from the desk and leans forwards, propping his elbows there instead. "So, let's talk changes." I pull out my notes, and he smirks. "You write?"

"I do a lot of things now I'm in charge."

His smile fades. "We spent so long thinking about this day, I don't think I ever believed it'd come."

"Don't get all sentimental on me, Grizz. You know I hate emotions." I open my notes. "New girls."

"Now, that's one I'm on board with."

"Put the word out we need ten girls in Zen. I want them clean, hardworking, and keen. Maybe go over to the Kings' patch and offer their girls a better deal."

"You want us to steal Kings girls?"

"I want you to offer them a better deal. We all know the Kings keep their girls clean. That's half the work done for us." The Kings are a rival MC on the other side of Manchester, but they're smaller than us and wouldn't bother to take us on over some pussy.

"You're the boss," he says, shrugging. "I'll put Duke and Ink on it."

"Next, I want that place cleaned out from top to bottom. We redecorate and get new beds, sheets, curtains, the lot."

"Costly."

"Did you see the state of the place? I wouldn't let my worst enemy's cock rub those sheets." He grins. "And add dishes to the list. I broke them all."

"What about Chas?" he asks. "Are we keeping her?"

I shake my head. "No. I've told her already. She cried and left. I've got someone in mind to take her place."

"Oh yeah, anyone I know?"

"Thalia."

He stares for a good minute, and I can see he wants to ask why I'd even think of getting my ex to run Zen, but he thinks better of it and nods. "Whatever you say, Pres."

"Put the prospects on decorating duty. I also want men stationed at each bookie's. There's to be no more credit. I want all debts paid in the next twenty-four hours. Track down those who don't pay and add twenty-five percent interest on for every day they're late."

"Got it," he says, standing. "I'll send the men out right away. Quick question—when are we celebrating?"

I arch a brow. "What are we celebrating exactly?"

"Being free, brother. It's been five years. It'll pick up morale around the place."

"We'll celebrate when this club is running how I need it to run," I say firmly, and he sighs, leaving.

"Fucking celebrate," I mutter to myself, slamming the notebook closed. I glance at the large portrait of my father, which he had painted when he first took over from my grandfather. "What do you reckon, old timer? Would you have partied instead of sorting the shit out?" I laugh to myself. "Of course, you would. Any chance for a celebration, which is why I'm cleaning your mess up now."

LEXI

I pace the office, sickness bubbling in the pit of my stomach. "You've got this," whispers Karen, and I glare at her. The men left to draw up some paperwork and find my handler. *A fucking handler.*

"I was told you wanted me on the force."

"And we do."

"Not undercover," I hiss. "I have zero experience. Is it even legal?"

She smiles. "Of course, it is. They've already run it through the proper channels, which is why they've gone to get the paperwork together."

"It's not going to work out. My mum hasn't seen me in years. What if she turns me away?"

"She won't. We have a plan for that."

I groan. "Of course, you do. Did Grace know about this?" My old sergeant was also my friend, and I refuse to believe she let me move here without telling me the truth.

"Nobody knows, and nobody can know. We don't know what contacts are trustworthy. The Chaos Demons are a big club, and they have too many people on their payroll."

"You're not helping," I hiss. "That just makes me wanna run away."

A man knocks before entering, and we both turn to look at him. He gives an easy smile. "Lexi," he says, holding out his hand, and I shake it. He reminds me of a social worker, a middle-aged man trying to act cool. "Jack Cole. Ex-undercover. I'll be your handler while you're out there."

"I haven't decided if I'll be out there just yet," I mutter.

He glances at Karen, who stands and excuses herself, leaving us alone. "Please, take a seat," he says, and I do. He sits next to me. "It's huge, right?" I nod. "And I get you're probably shitting yourself, but you can do this."

"I'm not so sure about that," I reply with an empty laugh.

"Do you wanna be a beat bobby forever?" he asks, sniggering.

"I like my job," I spit.

He sighs, trying a different tactic. "Not many people get this opportunity. The guys at the top obviously see something in you."

"Bullshit," I snap, standing again and moving over to the window. "They saw my past and realised I'm their way in."

He grins. "That too."

"I don't know anyone from the club," I say, even though I've already said all this to Smithe and Collinson. "I've not been there since I was a little kid, and I don't remember anyone. Not even names. I blocked all that shit out."

"The President goes by the name Axel. His father was before him, and his grandfather before that. Axel only just took over from his father, who died a few weeks ago, so we need to strike now while his head's fucked and his defences are down."

"So, when I was there, his father was the president?"

Jack nods. "Tank. He was well respected, although things have been slipping for a while. He couldn't cope with being ill and running things. He had Ice, his Vice President, helping, but rumours have it that he's useless and has caused the club a headache."

"So, why wasn't Axel the VP? Isn't that how it works?" I ask. Biker gangs aren't big in Nottingham, but I have some distant memory of how things ran back when I was small.

"He was in prison. Released this week." He pulls a file from his bag and lays it open on the table. "If you say yes, I'll start at the beginning."

"I'm not ready," I admit. "This is all moving too fast."

He nods, closing the file again. "How about we get out of here?"

Jack drives me to his place about forty minutes away from the station. We park up, and he dumps his bag in his house while I wait outside. Then we walk to the end of his road and into a bar.

"Welcome to The Corner Pub," he says with a grin as he pushes the door open.

Inside is old, reminding me of bars I went to with my mum when I was a child. The dark brown bar is sticky with unwiped spillages, and the carpets aren't much better. "This is on neutral territory," he explains. "No gang wars. It's peaceful, and I like how everyone keeps their heads down and enjoys their pints with no questions asked."

I take a seat in the corner while Jack goes to the bar and

orders us each a beer. When he returns, I take mine and gulp half of it down. "I think we need something stronger," he says, laughing. He goes back to the bar and returns with a bottle of tequila, some shot glasses, and two more beers.

"Why me?" I ask, pouring the tequila into the glasses.

"You know that already."

"Not really. How am I of any use when I don't know the club and I haven't seen my mum in years?"

"They're more likely to trust you cos you have history there. Your mum still hangs around the club, making it easier for you to get an in. Plus, Axel is shaking things up, and they're looking for new girls." He glances away, and I frown.

"New girls?" I repeat.

"To work for the club."

I narrow my eyes. "Doing what exactly?"

"You don't have to do anything you don't want to."

"I don't understand." Although, I think I do.

"Women hang around the place, hoping the guys will pick them to be their old lady."

"So, I've just got to hang around?"

He winces. "The women often resort to . . . sleeping their way around the club."

"Not a fucking chance," I say clearly. "No way." I drink the shot and pour a second.

"I have a plan for that."

I scoff. These pricks have a plan for everything. "So, first, you want me to approach my mum and hope she doesn't reject me for a second time. Then you want me to whore myself out to a bunch of criminals. For what?"

"Information. And I don't expect you to whore yourself out. You're taking it out of context."

"What makes you think they'll tell me anything?"

"They won't, but he might."

"Who?"

"Axel."

I raise my eyebrows in surprise. "You need me to get close to their president?" He nods. "And how do you suppose I get 'close' to him?" I ask, using air quotes.

"One step at a time."

I drink a second and then a third shot before drinking the second half of my beer. "Why don't you do it anymore?" I ask.

"I lost too much," he mutters, drinking his own shot, "but we don't have time to discuss me."

I shake my head. "I don't think so. If I'm gonna do this, I want to know everything about you. Everything."

He grins. "You're doing it?"

"Are you married?"

He shakes his head. "It's not the type of life that gives you time to be a husband or have kids. The job takes over, and it's easier to stay single, so you don't have to explain why you're gone for days on end."

"Great. Is that another reason I was picked, for my sad, lonely life?"

"You'd have to ask Smithe that one. I'm just here for you."

"What exactly happens once I go undercover?"

"I'll be your point of contact. You check in with me as often as you can and feed anything back to me. If you're unsure of anything or need permissions, you go through me. You never contact the station or anyone in it. That goes for Nottingham too. You can't risk them tracing numbers. They'll think you're a grass."

"What if they trace your number?"

"Simple. If they ever discover me, I'm your ex."

"An ex I still contact? Who does that?"

"You, apparently. If they ever ask about me, which they won't, I'll be Edward Jacks. That way, if you ever slip up, Jacks is still part of my name, and we'll say that's what my friends call me. I was your boyfriend in college back in Nottingham.

We can't change your story as they'll know you through older members and your mum. Stick to your real story as much as possible and add me in."

"Why did we split up?" I take another shot.

"You probably cheated," he says dryly, topping up both our glasses.

I grin. "Not my style. I'm a bit of a manhater, to be honest."

"You're gay?" he asks, surprised.

"No, straight, but men and I never seem to work out. That's why I threw myself into work."

"Winning two bravery awards," he teases, and I blush. "But seriously, you've got this, Lexi. You're well on the way to being the best of the best. This step will just get you to the top faster."

"Six months is what they told me. Is that still the case?"

He nods. "We hope so."

"I can do six months." I say it with purpose, but I'm not sure if I'm trying to convince myself or Jack.

"Then you can go home and pretend none of this happened. And watch the job opportunities roll in."

AXEL

The women file into the room in Zen and stand side by side. I run my eyes over each one, taking my time to appreciate each lace-clad curve. "Arms," I say, and they each hold out their arms so I can check for track marks. I nod to Grizz, who looks relieved. It's the second lot of women I've met—the first were a no-go, with either signs of drug use or they were too unclean looking.

"Ladies, you're hired," Grizz announces. "Go look around and get acquainted with the place.

They file out, and I pour myself a whiskey from the small bar we had built in the corner of the room. "Any sign of our new manager?"

"Yep, this is for Dutch courage," I tell him, knocking my drink back. "Thalia is on her way."

Minutes later, she appears, leaning in the doorway with a smug expression. "Axel," she says dryly, pushing past me to go inside.

"You look good," I tell her. It's not a lie, she's wearing a figure-hugging catsuit in red that clings to her slim frame but shows off her rounded arse and full breasts. I always loved her in red.

"I know," she says, looking around the room. "Where are your girls?"

"Upstairs looking around."

Her eyes land on Grizz as she makes her way through to the back room. "I see you're still thick as thieves," she says, air kissing him.

"Good to see you, Tali. Looking good as ever."

"Five years haven't been kind to you," she says, lowering onto the new pink plush couch. "I like the décor."

"It's all new," I tell her. "Like I explained over the phone, I need a relaunch to get it back out there, but with your help, I think it'll be a great little earner." Thalia's expertise in this area is second to none, which is why I swallowed my bitterness towards her and offered her the role as manager.

"We'll do a trial run," she announces. "Four weeks. If you fuck me over just once in that time, I'll walk."

"Okay," I agree.

"Keep your hands to yourself and stay out of my private life," she adds.

I nod. "Of course."

She eyes me for a second before extending her manicured hand for me to shake. I take it, ignoring the spark of electricity I feel. It's been too long since a woman touched me. "Deal. Now, leave, so I can meet the girls."

I step out with Grizz right behind me. "Fuck, she's an ice queen," he mutters, shuddering.

"Yep, some things never change."

"I don't know why you always go for women like her, Pres. Don't she scare the fuck outta yah?"

I laugh. "Until you've had an ice queen scream your name, don't judge."

"I don't imagine her screaming anyone's name," he mutters.

I slap him on the back. "Let's go. I need a stiff drink."

Back at the clubhouse a few minutes later, we head right for the bar, taking our usual spots and waiting for Shooter to serve us.

He places two glasses down and pours us each a whiskey neat. "You did good at Zen," I tell him, and he grins. "The place looks brand new."

"Cheers, Pres."

"How long you been prospecting for the club?"

"A year," he says.

"We'll talk about getting you patched in," I say, and his eyes widen in surprise.

Grizz waits until he's gone to serve someone else before turning to me. "Patched in, really?"

"He's a good lad, always ready to get his hands dirty."

"How the fuck do you know? We've only been back two weeks."

"I spoke to my father every day in his final months. We talked."

He lowers his head slightly. "Of course. Sorry, Pres."

"I don't do anything on a whim, Grizz. You should know that."

"We need something to lift the mood," he announces, standing and walking over to the juke box. "And where the fuck is all the pussy at?" he yells.

I snigger as Widow waves her hand in the air. She's been here for as long as I can remember, but she's good for the older members. "I meant someone half your age, Widow," he adds, shaking his head and grinning.

Seconds later, Cali appears. "I heard you boys want company?" She signals for London to join her, but she smiles shyly at me.

I stand, draining my glass. "Actually, I have shit to do. Have a good evening." And I head for my office.

LEXI

I take a deep breath as I approach the large metal gates. I don't remember the clubhouse looking like this, but I only have vague memories from back then. A man steps from the gatehouse, making me jump in fright. He looks me up and down. "Can I help you?"

My mouth opens and closes a few times before I sigh. "It's a long shot, but I'm looking for someone."

"Ain't here, sweetheart."

His rudeness instantly pisses me off. "You don't know who I'm looking for."

"Whoever it is don't wanna be found. Take a hint."

I frown. "You're fucking rude," I snap.

"And you're boring. Don't come back here."

"Fuck's sake," I mutter in a low voice. "I bet Tank doesn't know his men are so damn rude." I turn my back to walk away.

"What did you say?" he demands, and I smile before turning back and arching a brow.

"Tank. Your president."

He eyes me suspiciously. "Who did you say you were looking for?"

I stuff my hands in the pocket of my hoody. "My mum. Deborah Stevens."

He shakes his head. "I don't know no Deborah."

"Oh, she doesn't use her real name," I say, shaking my head like I forgot that detail. "Widow. She goes by Widow."

He nods one time before going back into the gatehouse. I wait patiently, and after a minute or two, I wonder if he's gone in there in the hope I'll leave. But then the door of the clubhouse opens, and a large man walks towards me. As he gets closer, I recognise him from the files Jack showed me as Shadow, the club's Enforcer. He looks me up and down. "Who are you?"

"Lexi," I say, trying to look more confident than I feel.

"And you say Widow is your mum?" I nod. "You poor fucker," he adds, shaking his head. "She ain't here right now. Can I ask her to call you?"

"Are you just saying that so I'll leave?" I ask, and he smirks. "I don't want any trouble. I just wondered if she wanted to see me. If she doesn't, I'll go."

He sighs. "Okay, I'll try and wake her. Hold on."

It's a further ten minutes before she finally appears. She steps outside and immediately shades her eyes from the dull skies. She's thinner than I remember, and it's clear the years haven't been kind to her. My heart hammers wildly in my chest as she carefully walks over, stopping the other side of the gate and staring at me. "Lexi?"

I nod, unable to form any words. I knew it'd be weird seeing her after all this time, but I wasn't prepared for the pain I'd feel. I stopped thinking about her so long ago, I thought I didn't care anymore, but turns out, I do. The little girl in me wants to scream at her for leaving me, and the adult in me wants to punch her in the face.

"You're here."

I nod again. "Seems so."

A tear wets her cheek. "Smoke, open the gate. Let the girl in," she says to the man in the gatehouse.

"Now, hold on, Widow, you know the Pres ain't happy about new faces."

"She's not a new face," Widow snaps. "She's my girl."

He groans but opens the gate anyway, and I step through. Relief floods me. I thought it'd be much harder to get inside, so completing this first step of my mission feels triumphant.

Once we get inside, memories of being in this exact room flood my mind. I look around, slowly turning and taking in the pool tables. I remember hiding under there when things got too loud. My heart slams harder in my chest as I remember seeing women's ankles with their knickers around them while they did shit with men I never understood until I got older.

I shake my head and zone back into my mum, who is excitedly telling another woman that I'm finally here. I give a weak smile, and the other woman returns it with her eyes full of pity.

"Come, let's get a drink."

I hesitate when she heads for the bar area. "Actually, a coffee would be great," I say, and she pauses, her smile fading slightly. "It's a little early for me."

She leads me in the other direction, and I take the opportunity to glance into the window of the door which clearly states 'President' in black lettering. It's empty. The only picture I've seen of Axel is his prison mugshot, and from that, I got that he was a well-built guy and good-looking, but it was taken five years ago, and those places can change you.

There're a couple younger women in the kitchen chatting

animatedly. When we enter, they settle down, watching me through curious eyes. "London, Cali, this is my girl, Lexi."

"I didn't know you had a girl, Widow," says London.

"We haven't seen each other in a long time," Widow replies, searching the cupboards.

"If you're looking for mugs, they're at the end," says Cali. Widow smiles at her in relief and goes to the correct cupboard, pulling out two mugs. "Coffee is above the kettle," she adds, then she stands. "We'll leave you to catch up. It's nice to meet you, Lexi," says Cali as they leave.

Widow eventually joins me at the table, but she avoids my eyes. "It's been so long," she mutters, and I can tell by the way she squirms in the chair, she's still using.

"Sixteen years," I confirm.

"Wow. Really . . . that long?" She almost looks sad.

"How have you been?" I ask, mainly to be polite because it's obvious she's been doing shit.

"Well, yah know, life seems to have passed so fast, I don't know where to start. What about you?"

"I'm good. Great, actually."

She smiles, showing her discoloured teeth. "That's really good. I always wonder about you. Are you married? Do you have children?"

I shake my head. "No."

"What brings you here to Manchester?"

I shrug. "I fancied coming back to see where I spent my early years."

She stares down at her fingers as she twists them together. "How's your dad?"

My skin bristles at her words. "Don't," I mutter. "Don't ask about him."

"Does he know you're here?"

I shake my head. "It's the one place he told me to stay away from."

"I'm glad you didn't listen."

I taste the coffee and wince at the bitterness. She notices. "Sorry, I don't often make it."

I want to bite out a response of sarcasm about how she never knew how to do anything normal, but Jack warned me to remain calm and not let emotions get involved, so I shrug, sliding it away.

"I should go," I say, pushing to stand. "I only came to see if you were still here . . . doing the same shit." I hang my head, regretting the last part. "Sorry, I didn't mean . . . never mind."

She stands too. "Are you sticking around?"

I shrug. "Maybe."

"Was it work or a man?" she asks, smiling. When I look confused, she adds, "That brought you here. It's usually work or a man that's an incentive to move."

"A man," I lie. "Sort of."

We make our way back through to the main room, and this time, the President's door is open and he's hunched over his desk, staring hard at a laptop. As I pass, he looks up, and for a second, our eyes connect and everything seems to slow down. I'm not sure if that's due to the fact I'm holding my breath and trying to slow my heart rate down.

He's gorgeous, better than the police mugshot, his shoulders are wide, and he's well-built. I imagine he spent a lot of his time in the prison gym to get that kind of shape. His beard is full and his skin tanned. *How the fuck does a prisoner get a tan?* But those things combined make his blue eyes stand out.

I force myself to look away, picking up my pace so I can get out of here. I didn't expect to feel anything, but there was definitely some kind of connection there, like I recognised him or maybe he recognised me.

"Wait," his gravelly voice barks from behind me, and I freeze, glancing at Widow for direction.

She winces and turns. "Pres, you remember my daughter, Lexi?"

I also turn but keep my eyes lowered. I'm terrified he'll recognise me from being a police officer, and if he knows that, this is over. I begin to panic as blood rushes around my body, causing a weird sensation in the tips of my fingers. White spots form in my eyes, and my ears fill with a whooshing sound.

"No, I don't," he snaps. "What the fuck is she doing in my club?"

"She came to see me," says Widow.

"I'm actually just leaving," I mutter, pointing to the exit. "Take care." I wince as I turn around to leave again. *Take care . . . why the fuck did I say that?*

"Take care?" he repeats, and this time, he sounds amused.

I don't bother to reply as I shove the door open and step out into the fresh air. "Will you come back?" asks Widow, rushing to keep up with me.

"I don't think I'm welcome. Do you?"

"Can I come to you?" she asks, and I see hope in her eyes.

"Sure." I pull out a piece of paper and a pen from my bag and scribble my address. "It's not far from here," I add, passing it to her.

I go straight home from the clubhouse, constantly looking around to see if I'm being followed. My mobile rings as I step through the door, and I press it to my ear. "You keep walking around like a nervous new kid and you're gonna get yourself either robbed or discovered," says Jack.

"You're watching me, you creep," I tease.

"Just doing my job. How did it go?"

"As far as first meetings go, it went well. I got in, which we didn't expect, right?"

"Nice."

"I don't think Axel was overly happy I was there, but he

didn't know until I was leaving, so I saved him the job of kicking me out."

"We expected that. He's not going to welcome anyone new into the club, which is why I thought you'd have been better trying to get in as a new club girl."

We'd spent an hour straight arguing the reasons why I was never going to make a good club whore. Plus, how the hell would I have gotten out of the sex part? Jack came up with all kinds of ideas, like telling the men I had an STD, or getting them so drunk, they couldn't perform. All sounded way too risky to me, and there was no way I was going to actually have sex. "Let's not go over that again," I complain.

"You get one shot, Lexi."

"Trust me on this. I spent the entire night reading his profile. He hates a walkover, and he doesn't touch the club whores."

"He's been inside for five years. He'll be a raging hard-on."

"He's too disciplined. He'll be hitting the gym hard and having cold showers."

"Or fucking his ex," he replies.

I frown. "Ex? I thought she was out the picture." His notes said she'd left the second he was sentenced.

"Apparently not. She's the new manager of The Zen Den." I laugh again at the mention of the club's whorehouse disguised as a massage parlour. It's a ridiculous name, and it makes me chuckle every time I hear it.

"There's an open evening tonight."

"No can do. I'm making friends tonight."

"Is that code for those dating apps where you slide into a man's DMs and meet for some shmexy time?"

I laugh. "Christ, you sound old. I'm meeting my friend's sister and her group. I thought it would be nice to have some friendly faces."

"Lex, that's a terrible idea," he says firmly, and my heart

sinks. "This job is going to consume you for the next six months. You have to become the person we're creating."

"I know, and she has friends."

"You're dragging people into something blind."

"Trust me when I say these people don't mix with bikers. I'll keep the two separate."

Jenna, Ben's sister, texted me instructions to meet her at a bar in town. I check the name on the text before entering the wine bar. We've only ever spoken through text message, but I spot her right away, waving at me frantically. The second I'm within grabbing distance, she throws her arms around me. "It's so great to finally meet you. How are you settling?"

"And you. So far, so good."

"Great. Let's grab a drink, and the guys will be here soon."

"Have you told anyone what I do?" I ask. "For a living?"

She shakes her head. "No, it hasn't come up."

"Great." Relief floods me. "Because no one can know. It's really important."

She eyes me for a minute. "Okay. Is everything okay?"

I nod. "Yeah. It's just this new role requires me to be very secretive."

Her eyes widen. "Oh my fucking god, are you undercover?"

My heartbeat quickens. "No, no, nothing like that. It's just, well, my mum's an addict, and I'd hate for anyone at the station to find out about her and vice versa. It's all just complicated, and besides, people are weird when you tell them you're a copper."

It's a lame excuse, and she frowns like she's not buying it but shrugs anyway. "Ben sometimes has that problem. My lips are sealed."

CHAPTER 3

AXEL

Lexi Cooper. I sigh heavily, remembering a time when she was just a small, scared little girl. I was eighteen when her father came and took her from Widow. It was the best thing that could have happened for the kid.

But she's not a kid anymore. She's the same woman that caught my eye when I was riding out the other day, when she was walking down the road looking fucking hot in tight jeans.

I take a deep breath and it brings me back to reality, back into the bar Thalia hired right next to Zen for the open event. She didn't want me to be here—of course she didn't. She spouted some crap about bikers scaring off potential clients. Fucking clients? Since when did men paying for sex become something posh? They're punters. Simple.

Grizz groans, dropping onto the stool next to me and clinking his glass with mine. "When can we get out of here?"

"Soon."

"Duke's gonna leave bankrupt. He's taken two of the women back to Zen."

"We'll give it half an hour then round everyone up. We can head out and leave Shadow to make sure it's a smooth evening."

The door opens, and I look up as Lexi steps into the bar. I frown and shake my head, wondering if I'm imagining her, seeing as she's been on my mind constantly, but she's right there as clear as day.

"Wow," mutters Grizz. "Now, that's what I call hot."

"She's Widow's daughter," I say, and I feel his eyes burn into my head. "Yep," I confirm. "She turned up at the club looking for Widow earlier today."

"Shit. How the fuck did Widow produce that beauty?"

I grin. "Back in the day, Widow was quite the looker. All the men wanted her."

"So I hear. No one ever took her, though."

"Yeah, well, the drugs got her first."

"What happened to the kid? Where she been all this time?"

I take a drink of my beer, keeping my eyes fixed on the brunette as she laughs at something one of her friends says. "Her dad rescued her when she was a kid. Best thing he ever did was get her away from the club."

"Widow never talks about a daughter."

"I'm surprised she even remembered, Grizz. She's spent her life on crack. The day Lexi left, she didn't shed one fucking tear. She shot up and moved to the next brother, business as usual."

"She looks like she turned out alright, though, and there's nothing to stop me—" He's about to go over there, but I put my arm across his chest to stop him. He frowns in confusion, and I'm just as confused, but I shrug it off.

"Let's not confuse shit at the club. We're just sorting through the mess, and we don't need to complicate anything."

"Who said anything about complicated?" he asks, winking. "You might be happy to go five years with only a wank for company, but I," he begins to walk in her direction, "need to feel a real pussy and not one that's had any of my brothers inside it."

I shake my head in annoyance. All I can hope is her dad taught her enough common sense to stay the fuck away from bikers.

I watch Grizz introduce himself and roll my eyes at her doe expression as the blush creeps across her cheeks. She's fucked, I think to myself, but then she does something unexpected. She scans the bar until her eyes find mine, and once again, we're locked in some kind of slow-motion movie scene where the bar fades into the background. I give my head a little shake. I don't know what the fuck happens whenever our eyes meet, but the pull is strong.

Grizz has moved on to chatting with her friend, and Lexi watches them, occasionally looking my way, but I'm not falling for it. I don't have time for a woman. Especially not Widow's daughter, who's at least ten years younger than me.

LEXI

I make eyes until I can't make eyes anymore, and still, he makes no move towards me. It was a coincidence we walked into this bar to find some of the Chaos Demons here. Once I realised, I tried to talk the girls into leaving, but they insisted on staying. I promised Jack I'd keep my two worlds separate, and here we are with the club's VP desperately trying it on with my new friends.

He eventually turns his charms back to me, despite me already giving him the brush-off. "You anything like your mother?"

Axel must have told him who I was. I arch a brow. "Is that your way of asking if I'm a drug addict or a whore?"

He grins. "I meant personality, but if you wanna confess

all your sins, sweetheart, I'm all ears."

I roll my eyes. "Who's the guy over there?" I ask, nodding in Axel's direction.

"Why're you pretending you haven't met him?"

"I never said that," I say, "but he didn't introduce himself to me earlier."

Grizz throws an arm around my shoulder. "That, sweetheart, is my President. But if you want any info on him, you can go ask him yourself."

"He doesn't look the type to talk about himself," I say.

He puts his fingers in his mouth and blows. The high-pitched whistle gets the attention of almost everyone, and he grins. "Pres, come over here. Lexi wants to know more about you."

My cheeks instantly burn with embarrassment, and I stare wide-eyed at Grizz. "Why would you do that?" I hiss.

He grins wider. "Aww, look how cute you are when you're embarrassed."

I feel him before I see him. He's practically pressing his front to my back, and I freeze, still glaring at Grizz with hatred. "What do you wanna know, Mouse?" Axel whispers in my ear, and the rumble of his deep voice causes my skin to prickle.

"I don't . . . I mean, Grizz was just . . . I don't want to know anything," I blurt, wincing at my embarrassing rambling.

"Are you single, free, and up for one night of fun?" Grizz asks him, laughing at my mortified expression.

"God, no," I gasp.

"You don't find me attractive, Mouse?" he asks, and I feel the smirk in his tone.

"Mouse?" is the only thing that falls from my mouth.

"Small, cute, wary of predators."

"Axel?" A woman's voice breaks our moment, and I feel

Axel pull back like he's been stung. "Isn't it time you and the monkeys were off now?"

I move to stand closer to Lola, one of Jenna's group, so I can watch the two converse. Axel looks irritated, but for whatever reason, he decides not to bite back with words I know he's desperate to say. Instead, he forces a smile. "Thalia, I was just coming to find you to say goodbye. We'll leave Shadow here to ensure the rest of the night runs smoothly."

"It will. I don't need your men making the place look untidy."

He inhales deeply for a second time, and I realise it's his way of staying calm. "Grizz, gather the men. Let Shadow know he's staying here until closing."

Grizz gives a head nod and rushes off to follow out the instruction. Thalia places her hands against Axel's muscled chest and stares up at him. For a second, a look of love passes over his face before he shuts it down. He kisses her roughly on the cheek and moves around her, heading for the exit.

Thalia turns her attention to me, looking me up and down in a way I'm sure she thinks is intimidating. "If I was you, I'd stay clear of Axel. He's not the sort of man you'll recover from."

I arch a brow. "Really? That sounds like the words of a bitter ex."

She narrows her eyes, suddenly aware I'm not the type you can scare off. "It's the words of a wise woman who chose to walk away from his cheating, lying arse. But, hey, if you want to go there, fine. Why should I care?" She flicks her long, shiny hair over her shoulder and stomps away.

"She's a barrel of fun," mutters Lola, and I grin.

"Let's get out of here."

Outside, Axel is chatting with some of his men. I catch his eye as we pass, and we share another intense stare-off. I think he's noticing me, and that's exactly what I need.

The following morning, I arrange to see Mum. Jack suggested me inviting her to my place, but I wanted to appear more natural, and if I really wanted to get to know her again, it's not something I'd do. So, instead, we meet at a coffee shop just around the corner.

She's late, and when she finally arrives, she looks tired and dishevelled and a lot more like the mum I remember. She sits and gratefully takes the coffee I ordered her. "You okay?" I ask.

"The tram was running late," she mutters.

"Tram?" I repeat. "The club's a short walk."

"I wasn't at the club last night. The men were out, and there's no point hanging around if they're not about."

"Oh. Where do you go when you're not at the clubhouse?"

She fidgets uncomfortably. "What have you been doing? Have you settled in?"

I allow the change of subject, and I'm about to answer when my mobile begins to buzz across the table. I immediately cancel Dad's call. He's been trying to get hold of me for the last couple days, but I hate lying to him, so I've resorted to texting him instead, telling him I'm too busy to chat.

Mum sees the caller ID and bites on her lower lip. "Does he know yet?" I shake my head. "Bet he warned you to stay away from me."

"Can you blame him?" I ask.

"He probably filled your head with lies," she adds.

I scoff. I'm trying to remain professional, but it's hard staying in character when this is also my real life. "He didn't need to—I remember a lot of things."

"You were just a kid."

"What are you up to today?" I ask, ignoring her comment.

"Not a lot. Why?"

"I've gotta go to the bank and withdraw some cash. Then we could grab some food."

She smiles. "Yeah, I'd like that."

We finish our drinks with chatter about what the area is like. Then she heads out to the bank with me, where I withdraw five hundred pounds. I feel her eyes glued to the cash. It must be hard for an addict to see that amount, which is what I'm counting on. I stuff it in my bag and then we head for lunch.

After we've eaten, I ask her back to mine so I can show her around the place. And while we're in the bedroom, I stuff the cash under my pillow.

"You know, you shouldn't have cash lying around," she says.

"It's to pay some bills," I lie. "Why don't you put the kettle on, and I'll just nip to the toilet," I say, shrugging out of my jacket.

I make sure to stay in there for some time before going to the kitchen, where she's sitting at the table with two coffees. My mobile rings again, and I decide to step out into the hall and take it, giving her extra time to take the cash because I honestly expected her to have left with it already.

"Dad," I answer. "Sorry I've been missing your calls. How are you?"

"Better now I'm hearing your voice. How's Manchester?"

"It's good. Same as Nottingham, just bigger."

"Have you made friends?"

I smile at his worry. "Yes, Dad, I've made friends."

Mum comes out into the hall with her coat on. She smiles and gives a small wave. "I have to go. Call me," she says as she leaves.

I nod, wincing and hoping to God that Dad doesn't recognise her voice. "Who's that?" he asks.

"A work colleague. She came for coffee."

"Right, well, don't let me keep you. Call when you get some time."

"Okay. I love you, Dad."

I rush back inside and lift my pillow. The cash is still there, and I frown as I put a call in to Jack. "She didn't take it," I say.

"Weird. Maybe she's a changed woman."

"Umm, I doubt that. Maybe it's cos it was too obvious it'd be her. I'll invite her over tomorrow for dinner. Maybe she needs time to think on it. The addiction will get the better of her."

I spend the rest of the day reading up some more on Axel. His prison report makes him sound like a saint. He kept his head down, was popular amongst the other prisoners, and he took parenting classes. I frown. Why the fuck did he take parenting classes?

I eventually tuck the files away in a loose floorboard and climb into bed. It's been a strange day, and although I have no interest in getting to know my mum, I didn't exactly hate seeing her today.

I wake sometime later with a start. Sitting up, I hold my breath because I swear, I heard a sound. I lean over to flick on the bedside lamp and scream when a hand covers my mouth, pinning me back onto the pillow. The man leaning over me has a balaclava on, and the only thing I can see are his steely dark eyes. Another man appears beside him, holding a metal bar. "Money," he barks.

My heart hammers in my chest. "I don't have any," I manage to squeak out.

The man holding me grabs a handful of my hair and pulls me from the bed, slamming me hard onto the floor. "Don't fucking mess with me," he warns. "Where the fuck is your money?"

"I don't keep any money here," I cry, not expecting the slap he dishes out. My cheek burns, and I place my hand over it. The other man begins to pull drawers open, throwing things on the ground as he searches.

"Make it easier on yourself," snaps the man looming over me. When I don't reply, he punches me hard in the face then lifts my head slightly and slams it on the ground. My vision blurs, and I squeeze my eyes closed, taking deep breaths to keep my impending panic at bay.

"Got it," I hear the other say, and then they both leave like this didn't happen.

I lay on the ground for a few minutes, fighting tears and going over what the hell just happened. My face feels like it has its own heartbeat. I carefully lift my fingers to it and feel swelling.

Pushing myself to sit, I wince when my head bangs in protest. I turn onto my knees and crawl through to the living room to check they've definitely gone. When I see it's empty, I crawl to the door and shove it closed before leaning against it, closing my eyes, and taking calming breaths.

When my head finally stops spinning, I push to stand and go back through to my bedroom to call Jack. He answers on the second ring, his voice croaky, and it's clear I've woken him. "Everything okay?"

"No. I just got robbed."

I hear rustling as Jack sits up. "What?"

"Two men, white, large build. They broke into my place and demanded the money."

"Was it coincidence, or do you think they knew?"

"I can't be certain. They didn't know where it was. They just found it after tipping my room upside down. But surely, it's not a coincidence I get robbed the exact same day I take cash out the bank and hide it in my room."

"Let's put the plan into place. What do we have to lose?"

"I'll go to the clubhouse first thing."

"Are you okay? Did they hurt you?"

I stare at my swollen eye and cheek in the bedroom mirror. "Nothing I can't handle."

CHAPTER 4

AXEL

I lift my foot, releasing pressure from Racer's neck. We've been at this for half an hour now, and the fucker's almost at a breaking point, I can feel it. He's from the Kings MC across the other side of town. Funnily enough, it was his President who called me to say he thought Racer was skimming money from one of my betting shops.

He gasps, and I give it a second before I place my foot back. He squirms beneath me, and when I lift it again, he cries out the name I've been asking for the last half-hour. I smile, satisfied that I was right. Giving him one last kick to the ribs, I nod at Shadow to deal with him.

When I go outside, Grizz is leaning against his bike. He lights a cigarette and passes it to me. "You owe me twenty," I tell him, taking it gratefully.

"Fuck, not Billy. He's been running that shop for over ten years."

"Pay up," I say, grinning as he dips into his pocket and pulls out a twenty, slapping it in my hand. "Let's pay Billy a visit."

"You know we have men to do this shit for us," he points out, throwing his leg over his bike.

I take a few deep drags of the cigarette before dropping it to the ground and mounting my own bike. "Where would the fun be in that?"

———

The bookmaker's is busy. There're a few races on today, and it's good to hear the tills ringing as people place their bets. One of the women behind the counter spots us and rushes off to the back office to announce our arrival to Billy. He's been running this shop for so long, it's disappointing we've got to this point.

He appears from the office looking flustered and panicked. He holds out his hand, but I don't shake it. "Axel, it's good to see you, son. I heard you got released."

"Shall we go somewhere quiet?" Grizz suggests.

"My office is free," Billy says, leading the way.

Inside, he rounds the desk and takes a seat. He probably thinks it gives him an air of importance. It doesn't—it just irritates me more.

Grizz places his hands on the other side of the desk and fixes Billy with a hard stare. "We've been hearing some tales, Billy. We thought we'd come direct to you and ask you straight." Billy begins to shake his head and mutter protests, but Grizz holds up a hand to stop him. "Let me just warn you that my Pres ain't like his father. He ain't fair and he won't listen to your bullshit. I'm advising you to speak the truth cos he fucking hates liars."

Billy swallows, glancing at me nervously. "Axel, I swear, I ain't done shit."

I sigh heavily. "How's the wife, Billy? She recovered after the cancer battle?"

His eyes lower until he's staring down at his hands. Understanding the veiled threat, he whispers, "Please, just hear me out."

"I'm gonna ask two things. I don't need an explanation, just a yes or no." He begins to whimper. "Do you know Racer from the Kings MC?" A sob escapes as he nods. "Are you in business with him?"

"It's not like that," he cries, and Grizz grabs a letter opener from the desk and stabs it in the centre of Billy's hand. Billy cries out in shock, and Grizz forces a piece of cloth into his open mouth to muffle the sound.

"Do you know how many times I hear that bullshit?" I ask, rounding the desk and resting my arse beside his bloody hand. "And it's always like that, Billy. Always." I take the letter opener and twist it. The wound will be much harder to close now. "How long?" I remove the cloth, and he sobs uncontrollably.

"Not long," he whimpers.

"Why you gotta make me do this shit?" I mutter, removing the letter opener. He cries out, pulling his wounded hand to his chest and cradling it with the other. I bring the opener down into his meaty thigh, and he yells a string of profanities. "We've spoken to Racer and got all the facts. So, get talking before I lose my patience and use this fucking letter opener to slit your damn throat."

"Okay," he cries, using the back of his good hand to wipe the beads of sweat from his forehead. "A couple months. Racer needed to clean some money. That's how it started. The amount got bigger and bigger, and then he was using that to place big bets."

"You forged the betting slips after the wins?" Grizz asks, and he nods again, sobbing harder.

"How much?" I growl. He shrugs, and I twist the weapon in his leg. He screams this time, and I slap my hand over his mouth. "Think," I hiss angrily.

"Half a million, easy."

I glare at Grizz, anger pulsing through me. "Where's your cut?" he asks.

Billy's eyes flick to the safe, and I pull him to his feet. "Open it," I order, which he does.

Grizz pulls out a black bag wrapped tightly around bundles of cash. "You fucking idiot," he mutters. "Why would you keep the evidence in the shop?"

"My wife doesn't know," he admits, paling with each word. This fucker is ready to pass out.

I shove him hard, and he falls to the floor, clutching his hand and thigh. "Get the fuck out this shop. You don't work here anymore."

We get back to the club and dismount our bikes. "What we gonna do about him?" asks Grizz. "We can't let him walk after what he's done."

"I'll give the order in a few days," I say. "Dad would've been pissed. He respected Billy."

"Knowing your dad was battling cancer while that shit took advantage of his absence. Prick."

"You think Ice knew?" I ask, and Grizz stares at me. "I know I shouldn't think like that but—"

"Pres, we gotta trust everyone in this club unless they prove us otherwise. If you were thinking it, you should've asked Billy while he was wailing like a fucking baby."

There's a commotion at the gate, and we both look over to see Lexi rattling the metal and yelling at Scooter. "What the fuck's this bitch want now?" I mutter, heading over with Grizz behind me.

"You don't like her?" he asks.

"I don't know why she keeps turning up where I am," I say.

"She looks like she's had a beating," Grizz notices, and I take in her swollen cheek and black eyes.

As we get closer, Scooter gives an apologetic shrug. "She keeps coming back, and I keep telling her Widow ain't here," he explains.

"Where the fuck is she?" Lexi screams.

"You wanna stop making noise?" asks Grizz firmly, and she listens, dropping her hands to her sides. "Now, explain."

"I need to see her," she says.

"Well, like Scoot said, she ain't here, so what do you want us to do about it?" he asks coldly.

"I think you're lying," she snaps. "Covering for her. Was it you?"

"Was what me?" Grizz asks.

She points to her face. "This. Did you come into my flat last night?"

I feel the anger radiate from Grizz. "Now, why the fuck would I wanna do that?"

"Money," she spits. "She's the only one who knew I had it."

I groan. "Whatever's going on between you and Widow has nothing to do with this club. We don't have your money, and my guys definitely didn't mess your face up like that."

"And I should trust you, should I?" she asks, her voice dripping with sarcasm.

"Open the gates," I tell Scooter.

"You sure about this?" asks Grizz. "Bitch is acting all crazy."

"You can wait for Widow to show up," I tell her, ignoring him. "We'll ask her about the money together."

I go ahead, knowing she'll follow because she's too wound up to walk away. Inside, I call out for London, and she appears from the kitchen looking flustered. I choose not to ask what she's been doing and instead instruct her to get an ice pack together.

I point to the couches, and Lexi sits down. We stay silent

until London returns with the ice pack, handing it to Lexi. "You wanna tell me what happened?" I eventually ask.

She looks much calmer as she nods. "Two men broke into my flat and took my money."

"How much?" Grizz asks.

"Five hundred."

"Why did you have that much in the flat?" I ask.

"None of your business," she snaps.

"What makes you think it's got anything to do with Widow?" Grizz asks.

Lexi winces when she presses the ice to her cheek. "She knew I had it. She came to the bank with me yesterday."

I pinch the bridge of my nose. "Why would you let an addict see that amount of cash?"

"I wasn't thinking, okay," she yells angrily.

"You wanna cool it," I warn, pushing to stand. "I don't get yelled at in my own damn clubhouse. Whoever took it, it's long gone now. What did the police say?"

"I didn't call them," she mutters.

"Why?" I demand.

"I thought you of all people would understand why I wouldn't call the police," she says, arching a brow.

"What the fuck's that supposed to mean?"

She lowers her eyes. "Nothing."

"You should go home and call them," says Grizz. "Let them deal with it."

"I can't," she mutters, keeping her eyes lowered. "I owe the money to someone."

"Who?" I ask.

"It doesn't matter," she snaps. "I just owe it, and I have until tonight to pay."

"Then tell whoever you owe that it's gonna be late."

"They wouldn't understand," she argues.

"Lexi, you've only just moved here, how are you in debt to someone?" I ask.

She stands, slamming the ice pack on the table. "Never mind. I wish I hadn't come."

Widow steps through the door just as Lexi is headed that way. She freezes, and Widow also stops dead, eyeing Lexi with concern. "Are you okay? What happened?" And I know from her expression she's lying—she knows exactly what happened to her daughter.

"I was robbed," says Lexi, fixing her with a sassy glare.

"Oh shit, and they did that to your face?" Widow innocently asks.

"My office, now," I bellow.

LEXI

Mum has a good poker face. It's how she's survived in life so long. I can smell the booze pouring from her skin, and she's way too bright to be hungover, which tells me she's happy about something else.

"Was this you?" asks Axel, glaring hard at her.

"Me?" she asks, adding an innocent laugh. "You think I had my own daughter robbed?"

"You used to make her sit out on the doorstep while you were fucking dealers for drugs," he snaps, "so, yeah, I do."

I gasp, wondering how he knows that, and then memories of me crying on the doorstep of Mum's house assault my brain. I frown. I'd forgotten about her house.

"Pres, I wouldn't do that. I've only just got her back."

"I really hope you wouldn't, Widow. It'd be a new low for you. Get out, let me talk to Lexi."

Once she's gone, he sits in his chair. "You forget about that?" he asks. "I heard you gasp."

I bite my lower lip, trying hard not to think about it. "I thought we'd always lived here, but I forgot she had a house."

"If that's what you can call it. It was a shit pit, and she didn't look after it. My father made her bring you to the clubhouse in the end. He thought it'd be safer for you."

"He did?" I ask.

"He was a sucker for a sob story."

"I don't really remember those days," I admit.

"Probably for the best."

"What happened to your dad?" I ask, chewing nervously on my lower lip like I have no clue that Tank is dead.

"He ain't around. He died." He sighs. "Why did you come back here, Mouse?"

I shrug. "I needed a change of scenery."

"If you've got any sense, you'll leave and go back home."

"Until I've paid this debt, I can't go anywhere. I don't want this to follow me back to my dad."

"I can give you five hundred." He stands and goes over to the safe, blocking my view as he inputs the number.

"It's more than that," I lie. "Maybe you can help me in other ways?"

He slams the safe closed and turns to me. "Like?"

"A job?"

He smirks. "What experience do you have?"

"I can turn my hand to most things," I say enthusiastically. "What sort of work have you got?"

He moves to me, taking my hand and pulling me to stand. It's unexpected, and I inhale sharply at the contact. My hand is so small in his. His other hand cups my cheek and tilts my head until I'm staring into his eyes. "That's a loaded question, Mouse. Which do you do better, fuck or dance?" And then he slowly runs his eyes down my body. Usually, this would piss me off, but I find myself wanting him to stare, to notice me.

"I don't do either of those," I mutter.

He grins. "You don't fuck?"

"I mean . . . I don't . . . no, I'm not . . . Oh god."

He laughs, taking pity on me. "You wouldn't last two minutes in this place. My men would eat you alive, literally. But I'll give you a trial now," he says, heading for the door. "Maybe you can prove me wrong." I frown but get up to follow.

He stops in the main room and pulls two tables together. He stands a chair next to them. "Your stage," he says, grabbing my hand and pulling me to the chair. He takes my waist in his large hands and lifts me effortlessly onto the tables. "What music do you prefer?"

"Music?" I ask, confused.

"Forget it, I'll choose." He taps away on the juke box, smiling to himself as a soulful tune plays out. Then he pulls up a seat and stares up at me. After a few seconds, he adds, "You can start when you're ready."

"Start?"

"To dance."

I shake my head. "I already told you, I can't dance."

"Everyone can dance, Mouse. How badly do you need the money?"

I bite down on my lip with nervousness. This could be my only chance at getting into this godforsaken club, so I take a deep breath and begin to sway my hips. I have the worst balance and absolutely no rhythm, so I'm not surprised when I glance his way to see him wincing.

"Foxy," he yells, and a woman comes rushing over. "Get up there and do something," he tells her.

She smiles at me, using the chair as a step and joining me on the tables. She stands behind me and places her hands on my hips, slowing down my jerky sidestepping. "Keep the feet still," she instructs. "Just sway with the hips." She begins to count in my ear, tapping me to sway one way then the other.

After a few seconds, she takes my hand and guides my arm up in the air. "Now, dip slow."

"How?" I hiss.

She laughs, moving to my side and showing me. I follow her, bending at my knees and dipping, before swooping back up gracefully. At least, I think it's graceful. "Start slow," she tells me. "Remove the outer layer first. Don't touch your underwear until towards the end of the song."

"I can't take my clothes off," I say, my eyes widening in fear.

"That's kind of the point," she says with a laugh. "It's fine. Axel's seen plenty of naked women, he won't judge."

"I've never done anything like this."

"Look, sweety, this ain't my audition, but if you want a job, you better get moving. Axel can get bored real quick."

I glance at him, and he's watching me through curious eyes. I climb down from the table so only he can hear me. "I'm a little nervous," I tell him.

"Fine, forget it. You know the way out," he says, standing. He begins to head back to his office.

I groan, rushing after. "No, wait," I cry, and he slows. "Maybe I can do a private dance first," I mutter, glancing around. "Away from all these eyes."

He sniggers. "Mouse, these men see tits all the time. Yours ain't anything special. But sure, whatever." He holds his office door open wider, and I go through. Once we're inside, he sits on the couch. "You know, you gotta get over this shy thing pretty quickly if you wanna earn cash."

"I will," I mutter, standing awkwardly. "I just don't have much . . . experience."

He laughs. "Undressing?"

"No, being naked around men," I admit, hating the words as they fall from my mouth.

He stares for a few seconds, choosing not to comment further. "Whenever you're ready."

"I don't suppose you have music in here?" I ask carefully, and he rolls his eyes. "Of course not, I'll just start," I mutter.

I begin to hum, and he narrows his eyes. "What are you doing?"

I chew my lip again. "I thought it might help me to relax." I take a breath. "Let's just get it over with."

"Please do," he mutters, pinching the bridge of his nose again.

I lift my top, swinging it over my head and releasing it. It sails through the air like a mini parachute and whacks Axel in the face. He snatches it away, glaring at me. "Sorry," I whisper. "Too much umph."

"A good dancer can make hundreds in one night," he tells me dryly. "You'll be lucky to make a two-figure sum at this rate." His eyes fall to my off-white bra that's been washed one too many times with my dark clothes. "What the fuck are you wearing?"

I glance at it and shrug helplessly. "I didn't know I'd be showing anyone."

"It doesn't matter, Mouse. That thing should never see the light of day again."

I ignore him and shimmy out of my jeans, groaning when I see the granny-sized knickers I chose to wear this morning. "Comfort," I say feebly.

"Christ, they don't even match the bra."

"Look, I clearly wasn't expecting to get naked in front of you today or I'd—"

"Today?" he repeats, arching a brow. "Were you planning on getting naked for me in the future?"

I feel my cheeks redden. I never get embarrassed, yet this biker's made me blush more than once. "No . . . I was . . ." I groan, covering my hands with my face. I hear the door open and uncover one eye to see Grizz staring at me with a smirk on his face.

"Sorry, am I interrupting something?" His eyes track over my body, and he grins. "What the hell are you wearing?"

I grab the jeans that are halfway down my calves and tug them up. "Forget it, this was a stupid idea," I mutter, fastening them.

"Hey, don't stop because I'm here. I can't wait to see where this is going."

"She needs work," Axel explains. "This was her chance to show me what she's got."

"You can't stick her in Zen. She won't last a day."

"Hey, I can massage a few backs," I snap, pulling my top on. They exchange a smirk. "It is a massage parlour, right?" I ask, giving my best innocent face.

"We only take on experienced masseuses," says Axel. "You can't dance, you can't fuck—"

"Shit, how did we find that out?" asks Grizz. "And why wasn't I invited?"

"I'm going off her own admissions," Axel tells him. "I have no reason to doubt her after her dance performance."

"Okay, so now we all know I'm useless, thanks for the recap. I'll get off," I say, heading for the door.

"Wait," Axel barks, and I freeze.

"Can you pull a pint?"

I slowly turn to face him with a confident smile in place. I'd worked in a bar when I turned eighteen while I trained for the police force. "I can pull a pint, mix a cocktail, and break up a brawl."

He arches a brow. "I'd like to see that when my men get rowdy. You got yourself a trial shift in the bar. Go out there and tell Shooter. He'll show you the ropes."

CHAPTER 5

AXEL

"I'm worried about you," says Grizz, placing a drink down in front of me.

I drag my eyes away from Lexi. "Why?"

"You've been inside for years, you've not touched a club whore since you got out, and you just watched a woman get half-naked in your office and didn't bend her over the desk to fuck her. If you're gay, I won't change towards you."

I laugh. "I ain't fucking gay. And I'm not sticking my dick inside any of those whores when they fuck anyone who asks. Lexi's younger than us. There's gotta be at least ten years."

"Eleven . . . I asked. Why do you care about age? She's an adult."

I laugh. "She wears knickers up to her tits." Grizz laughs loudly too. "And she's Widow's daughter."

"And that's why you gave her a job that wasn't even available," he says, knocking back his whiskey.

"I wanna patch Scoot in. He can't work the bar forever."

"So, we get a new prospect. Or we give Smoke more duties. He's been on bike wash for the last few weeks."

"Get off my case, would yah," I mutter. "I've got history with Lexi."

He sits straighter. "You fucked her?"

"No," I snap, narrowing my eyes in his direction. "She's too young for me. But I remember her as a kid, and she had a shit start in life."

"Fine, I get you wanna help her, even though I've never witnessed your conscience before, but did you find out who her debt is to at least, so we know what kind of shit she's in?"

"I'll get to that."

"What if it comes back on the club?"

"We'll deal with it."

"For a chick you don't know anymore? Pres, no disrespect, but she could be anyone now. She's been gone for years, so who knows what she's in to. And who moves to a place where they don't know anyone and don't have a job?"

"This is Lexi we're talking about. She wears ugly underwear and can't fucking dance. She's harmless. And she's the daughter of a whore who's been around this place since my grandfather ran it. Relax, Grizz."

"You're the boss," he says, shrugging. "But if she's too young for you, can I have a go? Cos them big knickers got me intrigued."

I roll my eyes. "Sure, whatever." But even as the words fall from my mouth, I wanna take 'em back.

LEXI

By the time I get home, I'm exhausted. Jack calls back at ten p.m., like I told him to, and I flop down onto my bed and answer. "Tell me you're in there," he says. I'd texted him earlier to say I had good news.

"Yep. The plan totally worked. I went there kicking up a fuss, and he invited me. I won't even tell you how embarrassing my day was, but I'm in. He's got me working the club's bar."

"Well done, Lex. That's brilliant. Do a few shifts and we'll start the next part of the plan."

"Okay."

"Remember to keep your eyes and ears open at all times. They'll talk when they think you're not listening."

"I know," I reply, smiling. "We've been over that."

"I'll report back. Well done. Sleep well." I disconnect and snuggle into my pillow. I haven't even bothered to change out of my clothes, and now, I'm too tired to move.

The week passes in a blur. I work every hour they ask me to, but I hardly see Axel or Grizz. None of the men speak out about either of them and they give nothing away. Jack puts in the next part of the plan, which means I'm getting another black eye, but at least this time, it's expected.

Jack wrings his hands together. "Are you ready?" he asks. I nod, bracing myself. "I should've just paid someone to do this," he mutters, shaking his head. He turns sideways to me, bringing his elbow back and quickly slamming it into my face.

"Fuck," I cry, clutching my face.

He immediately turns me in his arms and brings me to him, holding me against his chest. "Shit, are you okay?"

"You just hit me in my eye, of course I'm not," I say. I shake it off, and he releases me.

He produces a tissue and some fake blood. "Put the call in."

"What if he asks how I got his number?"

"Say Widow gave it to you. She's high most the time, she won't remember."

"Won't he wonder why I asked for it?"

"Jesus, I don't know. Say it's for work purposes. He is your boss."

I press call and wait for him to answer. When he does, he sounds irritated. "What?"

"Axel, it's me, Lexi."

"Lexi?" I hear him move around. "How did you get my number?"

I give Jack an 'I told you so' look and turn away from him. "My mum gave it to me. I thought I should have it in case I couldn't come into work."

"That's hard to believe, Mouse, when Widow doesn't have my number."

I wince, panic filling me. "Okay, I stole Scooter's phone and got it from there. I'm not proud."

"Are you calling for a reason?" he asks.

I'd forgotten the whole reason, along with how I was supposed to sound upset. "The man came back."

"What man?"

"Who robbed me. At least, I think it was him. He asked for more money, only I didn't have any."

"Are you okay?"

"Not really. Can I come to the clubhouse? I'll take the couch. I just don't feel safe here right now."

He hesitates. "It's not a good idea, Mouse. I'll get you a hotel."

My heart sinks. "No, it's fine. Sorry if I disturbed you." I disconnect before he can respond.

"He's cagey," says Jack.

"He doesn't trust me enough," I mutter, and the thought bothers me. "I'll find another way in."

"It's just gonna take time. I knew we shouldn't have rushed it."

"Now, I have another black eye," I say with a small laugh.

"I'll get the ice."

I sit on the couch just as the rumble of motorbikes slows outside. I rush to the window to see two bikers with Chaos

Demons kuttes dismounting. Jack runs in and asks, "Is that him?"

I shrug. "Hard to tell. He's got a helmet on."

Jack thrusts the fake bloody tissue at me and whacks the ice pack on my bruised eye. "Remember, I'm Edward," he hisses.

When the door buzzes, I answer. "It's me," says Axel in his gruff voice, and I can't help the smile.

"I thought you were busy."

"Open the damn door."

I release the lock and then open the door to my flat. Seconds later, he walks in, filling the doorway and making the place look a lot smaller. He removes his helmet, tucking it under his arm. The biker behind him does the same, and I see it's Shadow. I find him the most intimidating out of everyone. He hardly speaks, but I feel like he's constantly assessing everyone and making judgements.

Axel grips my chin in his fingers, turning my face up to the light to exam it. "Ice pack," he says, holding out his hand.

Jack places it in his palm, and Axel walks me back until I sit on the couch. He places his helmet beside me and holds the ice to my face. "You got a habit of getting yourself hurt, Mouse."

"Not by choice."

"Who's the geek?" he asks, still not looking at Jack.

I smirk. "Edward."

"You can leave now, Edward," he says firmly.

"I think that's up to Lexi," says Jack.

Axel arches a brow at me, waiting for me to say the words. "I'm fine, Edward. Thanks for coming down to check on me."

Jack grabs his jacket. "No problem, Lex. Anytime." He then moves between me and Axel and leans down, placing a lingering kiss on my forehead. When he pulls back, he winks before leaving.

"How the fuck did he get here so quickly?" Axel asks. "I was literally around the corner."

"He lives upstairs," I say, shrugging.

"Boyfriend?" he asks, sounding pissed.

"No."

"Why'd yah call me if he was here?"

"I called him after you because I didn't think you'd come."

He eyes me for a few seconds. "Get your shit together."

"I can stay at the clubhouse?" I ask.

"Hurry. I've got shit to do."

I rush to grab a bag and stuff some clothes inside. I can't believe it actually worked. I'm in.

CHAPTER 6

LEXI

The clubhouse is quiet when we arrive. I scan the room for Mum, wondering how she'll feel having me around. "We ain't seen Widow in days," mutters Axel, answering my unasked question. He hands my bag to Scooter.

"Is that usual, for her to just go off radar like that?" I ask.

He shrugs, not looking concerned as he lights a cigarette and inhales deeply. "Follow the prospect. He'll show you to a room."

I'm taken to the second floor, and as we walk along the passage, Cali appears from one of the rooms. She smiles, looking pleased to see me. "Hey, what are you doing up here?"

"I'm coming to stay."

"How come? Thought you had a place?"

Scooter opens a door a few rooms up from Cali and dumps my bag on the bed. Cali sits beside it. "I do," I tell her, "but I've been having problems with locals."

She gives a knowing nod. "Widow's fault. Grizz told me she had someone break in your place."

It's a half-truth, so I nod. "Axel said she's been MIA for a few days."

Cali shrugs. "Widow goes off radar a lot. The guys don't really bother too much. She's not exactly in demand these days. Anyway, once she finds out you're staying here, she'll probably turn up. How long you here for?"

"I'm not sure. Axel didn't really say."

"Welcome to the whores' halls of residence," she says, laughing. "We're all on this floor."

I frown. "You don't think . . . will I have to have sex with the guys?"

"Did you ask Axel the terms?" I shake my head. "Perhaps you should."

———

I unpack the few clothes I brought with me and head down to find Axel. He's hunched over his desk, staring at his mobile phone. I knock on the door, and he glances up. "Yeah?"

"I just wanted to clarify some things," I say, stepping in farther.

He sighs and places his mobile down then leans back in the chair, eyeing me warily. "You've been here less than an hour and you wanna lay down the law?" He arches a brow.

"No, nothing like that. It's just Cali said the floor I'm on is the whores' halls of residence." He laughs at that piece of information. "So, I thought I should check out the terms of my stay."

He rubs his jaw, all the time keeping his eyes fixed on me. "Like a hotel kind of thing?"

"What do you expect from me?"

Realisation passes over his face, and he smirks. "I've seen you dance, Mouse, and you showed me your underwear. Ain't no man here gonna visit you for a fuck. Relax." I'm mildly insulted, and my face must show it because he laughs again. "Now, you're offended?"

"You caught me on a bad underwear day."

He grins. "Yeah? What'yah wearing today?"

I bite my lower lip, knowing I'm wearing the same kind of thing. "I go for comfort."

He laughs harder. "Look, Mouse, you work the bar, help out around the place, and all will be good. Find Nelle—we call her Duchess—she's in charge of the kitchen and shit. She'll tell you what needs doing."

I leave the office and go to the kitchen, where I find a woman around the same age as my mum. "You must be Lexi?" she asks as she slices chicken.

"Axel sent me to find Duchess."

"Then you found her," she states, using the knife to point to a stool. I sit down. "You work the bar already, right?" she asks, and I nod. "I don't go out there, the guys get too rowdy, but I hear you're good with them."

"I'm still getting to know everyone. I've only worked here a week."

"They've all had good things to say. Hard to believe you're related to Widow, though."

"Yeah, we're completely different."

She smiles. "Good. I've got everything under control in here, so go and help in the bar tonight. Dinner will be at six. Breakfast is at eight. If you miss any mealtimes, there's always extra in the fridge, so help yourself. I could always use a hand at lunchtime. Find me tomorrow around eleven-thirty and I'll show you what I usually do around here."

I go back into the main room, where Cali is sitting on the couch with a couple club girls and Duke. She waves me over, and I sit down. "You remember Duke?" she asks, and I nod. "And London," she adds, and London gives a little wave. "And this is Fable." The other woman is like a pixy, small and cute, with the biggest green eyes. I've never seen Fable before, but working in the bar means the only time I interact with the club girls is when they're getting drinks for the men. Once they're in the bar, they're all about the men.

"Lovely to meet you," I say, and she gives a cute grin.

"She doesn't speak much," London explains as she shrugs, rolling her eyes. "Part of the mystery, apparently."

"Are you staying around for long?" Duke asks, finally looking up from his mobile phone. I swear, all the men here are glued to the things.

"I'm not sure."

"Are you available while you're here?" he asks.

"No, she ain't," snaps Axel, appearing from behind me. "Fuck, Duke, not every woman is a whore."

"Sorry, Pres, was just asking. The guys wanna know."

"Which guys?" Axel demands. "You're all like dogs in heat."

"You can't blame us, Pres. It's been too long since we had fresh pu—"

"Lexi, go work the bar," Axel snaps, cutting Duke off.

Scooter hands me the cloth as I step behind the bar. "Thank fuck you're here, I got shit to do," he says, stepping out and leaving me to it.

As usual, Cash is sitting at one end of the bar with his newspaper open and a half-drunk pint in front of him. He's often here, minding his own business.

Cali picks a stool at the opposite end, and I go over with her usual soda water. She leans closer.

"The Pres gave Duke a right earful after you went. He never does that sort of thing, especially in front of us."

"I cleared up my role with him, so he was probably just making it clear to the men."

"I should give you the rundown on everyone," she says, and I nod eagerly. I definitely need the information. "I'll start with the girls, because if you want a nice peaceful life, you have to keep them on side. Fable talks, just not when the men are around. They like that shy thing she's got going on. She's actually really clever, and her parents think she's an accountant. They have no idea she stays here and fucks around. Duke has a soft spot for her and buys her loads of nice stuff. London is a hard-faced cow, but she'll always have your back. She doesn't take shit, and the guys don't bother to give her any—she'd make their life hell. Foxy works at the massage parlour."

I hold my hand up to stop her, not wanting to miss the opportunity to find out more about the club's businesses. "Is it really a massage parlour?" I already know the answer, but I have to seem curious.

"Of course not. Those places don't exist unless it's run by the NHS. Anyway, Foxy spends a lot of time there. She's quiet and calm, always good at talking the guys down."

"What about the guys? I don't know any of them really, apart from Scooter."

"Grizz is the VP. He's a beast in the bedroom and a hard-faced bastard out of it. I see why Pres made him VP. He's your go-to for most shit that Duchess can't sort. If you bypass him and go right to Pres, he'll be pissed. He looks after Axel, and he takes his role seriously."

"Speaking of Axel," I say, wiggling my brows just as London joins us.

"What's going on?" she asks.

"Lexi wants to know about the Pres."

London arches a brow. "No disrespect, new girl, but you don't stand a chance."

I feel myself blush, and Cali elbows her. "That's rude."

London shrugs. "I'm being honest. Since he got out, he's not been near any of us. We all know he's waiting on Thalia to take him back."

"Thalia?" I repeat. "I think I met her."

"She's hard to forget. Bitch, but fucking stunning,"

London says, and I laugh. "The Pres loved her, and he's not bothered with anyone since she came on the scene."

"Ladies, ain't there enough cock to suck around here?" snaps Grizz, and both women jump off the stools and rush away. He takes their place. "Whiskey, neat."

"Please," I say, giving a smile before grabbing the bottle and a glass.

"You feeling at home?" he asks, taking the glass as I pour his drink. He holds his hand up when it's half-full.

"It's weird. I don't really remember all this from when I was little. I thought I would."

"What brought you back, Lexi?" he asks, taking a sip and keeping his eyes trained on me.

I shrug. "I guess I wanted to reach out to my mum."

"Why after all this time? You're an adult."

"Is there an age restriction on finding your useless parent?"

He taps the bar with his free hand, and I have a sickening feeling in my stomach that tells me he's doubting me. And from what the girls said, I've got to get him on side, or I'll never find anything out.

I lean closer, making sure he gets an eyeful of my chest. It works, and his eyes glance down before going to my lips. I smile sweetly. "Maybe I wanted to see what was so alluring about this life that she chose the club over me."

"Sounds like you got some issues there, sweetheart."

"Maybe you can help me out with those."

A smile pulls at his lips. "Maybe."

"I need you to drive over to Zen." We both look to Axel as he walks over. He looks annoyed, and I grab my cloth and move away. Something tells me his anger is aimed at me. "Thalia called. They've had some trouble."

"Can't you send Shadow?"

"I'm sending you," he barks. "Get gone."

Grizz rolls his eyes and slides from the seat. Axel replaces him and fixes his eyes on me. "What can I get you?" I ask politely.

"I didn't let you stay here so you could flirt with my men," he snaps. Even Cash glances up in confusion. "You wanna do that, I can change your job title to club whore."

"I was just being friendly," I mutter. "That's the job of the barmaid."

"No, Alexia, that's the job of a club whore. You serve drinks. Now, get me a beer." I resent his frosty attitude, and when I grab the beer, I slam the fridge door. He arches a brow. "You got a problem, Mouse?"

I place the beer in front of him without a word, and as I go to step away, he grabs my wrist. Two things happen—my heart slams hard in my chest, and my breathing hitches because I'm surprised by his sudden touch. And something passes between us. Something I've never felt with anyone, especially not a man I hardly know. It's like a warmth that spreads up my arm and wraps around my fast-beating heart.

We both stare at where his fingers gently hold my wrist, which looks so small in his large hand. "You got a problem, Mouse?" he repeats, bringing his eyes to my own.

I shake my head, not daring to speak because I know my voice will come out in some kind of embarrassing squeaky shrill. "Cos you know, all you gotta do is say the words and I'll make that change."

I take a breath to calm myself then square my shoulders. He lets my wrist fall from his grasp, and a smirk replaces his heated gaze. "Do you want me to be a club whore?"

He bites the corner of his lip, holding it between his perfectly white teeth, and runs his eyes down my body, slowly dragging them back up until they meet mine again. It's the hottest thing ever, and I almost gasp aloud. "Mouse, you ain't ready for what I can do to you."

I arch a brow to hide the fact this guy is charming his way into my knickers. For a second, I almost forget why I'm here. "Really? I heard you don't fuck around with the women here."

He grins, leaning back in his chair and shrugging. "You asking around about me?"

"Just trying to get to know my employer."

"Then come direct to me, cos no one can answer your questions better than I can."

"Noted," I say with a small smile, then I walk away to clear some glasses. He needs to work a little harder for my attention or he'll get bored.

AXEL

I can't seem to drag my eyes away from her. Lexi must sense it because, occasionally, she glances at me before quickly looking away. It only adds to the alluring pull she's got over me. My cock strains so hard in my jeans, it's painful.

"What were you inside for?" she suddenly asks, leaning her perfect backside against the counter while she wipes a glass.

"Why do you wanna know?"

She shrugs. "Curious."

"What do you think I was inside for?"

She pouts her lips, and I almost groan in pain imagining them around my cock. "Theft," she says, and I laugh. She smiles. "No? Okay, so maybe fraud?"

"Assault," I tell her. "Along with a few minor things."

She places the glass and towel down and leans her elbows on the bar, looking directly at me. "On a male or female?"

"You got me down as a woman beater, Mouse?" I ask. "I'm insulted."

"What did he do to deserve a beating?" She suddenly feels

a lot closer, and if I just moved my head forward a little, our lips would meet.

"You tell your ex you're staying here?" I ask, changing the subject.

She shakes her head. "I didn't tell you he was my ex. And no."

"You didn't need to. I saw the way his eyes were glued to you. He didn't like you calling me for help. Won't he be worried?"

"Why do you care?"

"I don't. How long were you together?"

She smirks. "Tell me about Thalia."

It was the wrong thing to say, and I sit back, putting space between us. "Who the fuck told you about her?" I snap, unable to hide my irritation.

Her smirk fades, and she pushes off the bar, snatching up the towel and wiping another wet glass. "Forget it."

"Don't poke around in my private life, Mouse. I don't fucking like it."

"I didn't poke around," she snaps, taking me by surprise. I can't deny the thrill I feel whenever she gives me attitude. "Christ, you ain't all that, yah know." She scowls. "Thalia warned me off you when I saw you in that bar. I just assumed you two were a thing."

"If you thought that, why the fuck are you flirting with me?"

She looks even more outraged. "That wasn't flirting."

"Whatever you say, Mouse. But I'm pretty sure if I'd have leaned in to kiss you just then, we'd be fucking in my office right now."

Her face burns red with embarrassment. "Actually, I prefer my men a little less . . . rough."

I grin. "That's cos you ain't tried it."

Before she can respond, my mobile rings. I press it to my

ear, winking at Lexi before turning away from her to speak to Grizz. "Pres, you gotta get down here. Thalia had a visit from Nick Matthews. He was trying to push the drugs in Zen, said he had permission."

When I step inside Zen, Thalia greets me with a hard slap, and I curse, wincing. "I thought this place was clean," she screams. Fuck, I don't miss her Italian temper. I grab her throat and push her against the wall, levelling so our eyes meet.

"Sweetheart, we ain't fucking, so there ain't a need for the kinky foreplay. You get me?"

"I won't run a place filled with your drugs," she spits, trying to fight me off.

I pin her tighter and feel Grizz behind me. "I'm gonna let you go, but you hit me a second time and I'll cut your fucking hands off." I push away, and she grasps her neck, glaring at me with hate in her eyes.

"He made threats," Grizz tells me, following me into the room where some of the girls are lounging around. "Said he's coming back later to burn the place to the ground."

"Sounds like a toddler tantrum," I mutter, eyeing Fable, who's smiling up at me with those big eyes. The temptation to get my dick wet is overwhelming, so I stomp back out the room and into the reception area, where Thalia is now sitting. "What did he say?" I ask.

"That he always sells here, and that isn't stopping because some prick in a leather jacket reckons he's a king around these parts," she says with a smirk.

I roll my eyes. "I'll pay him a visit," I tell Grizz.

"You want me to get some men together?"

I shake my head. "Nah, I need a release. I'll handle it."

He shakes his head in exasperation. "Not without me, you won't," he mutters.

Nick Matthews is a shady fucker. We spend half the night trying to find him, but he's always moving. We eventually track him to a nightclub. I watch him from across the dancefloor as he glides between bodies, occasionally stopping to slip something into eager hands.

"Christ, he's like a fucking slimy piece of shit handing out candy," Grizz mutters in my ear.

As he moves closer, I stand taller. I want him to see me watching. When he finally glances my way, he does a double take before arching a cocky brow. He waltzes over with the confidence of an idiot thinking he'll be able to threaten me. I don't give him a chance to speak before I have his neck in my hand and I'm shoving him hard against the wall. "What the fuck is this I hear about you not only disrespecting my business but also me?"

"Relax, we're both here to earn a living," he coos.

"Are you fucking high right now?" I growl, squeezing his throat tighter until he begins to go red in the face. "I don't want your shit in my place."

He pats my arm, and I release a little pressure. "We can come to an arrangement," he says.

"This is the arrangement," I snap, applying pressure again. "You stay the fuck away from anything to do with the Chaos Demons." He rolls his eyes, and I look to Grizz, hardly believing the guy's this dumb.

"He ain't listening, Pres."

"No, he ain't," I mutter, grabbing his collar and marching him from the nightclub.

Once outside, I shove him away from me, and he turns to face me in a stance that says he's looking to fight. I laugh hard. "Does this kid know who the fuck I am?" I ask Grizz.

"Yeah, well, I'm somebody too," Matthews yells back.

He looks past me to the doormen, who all turn their backs. I arch a knowing brow and smirk. "Really?"

"I can sell where the fuck I want. I have a deal with your VP," he yells.

I turn to Grizz, who shrugs. "This is my VP, and he don't know what you're talking about."

"Not this clown," he growls. "Ice."

Somehow, I knew that name would come up on a list of bad deals, and I shake my head slowly. "The deal's off. Ice isn't the VP no more, and Tank is dead. We run the club now, and all deals go through us."

"So, let's talk. Let's sort a new deal."

"I don't deal with pricks like you," I mutter, turning to walk away. I glance back when I hear a scuffle and see Grizz trying to hold Matthews back. I roll my eyes at his persistence. "You'd be a fool not to walk away while I'm giving you the chance," I tell him.

Grizz groans and releases Matthews, who takes off running in the opposite direction. Grizz then drops slowly to his knees, and as I move closer, he's holding his hand to his stomach. "Fucker got me, Pres," he says, pulling his hand away to show me blood.

"Fuck," I mutter, hooking his arm around my neck and pulling him to stand. "I'll get one of the brothers to pick him up. Let's get you looked at."

"No hospital," he mutters. "You know they'll call probation and I'll end up back inside." He's right. We're both on probation for the next few months, and they'll take one look at this and think we're back in trouble.

CHAPTER 7

LEXI

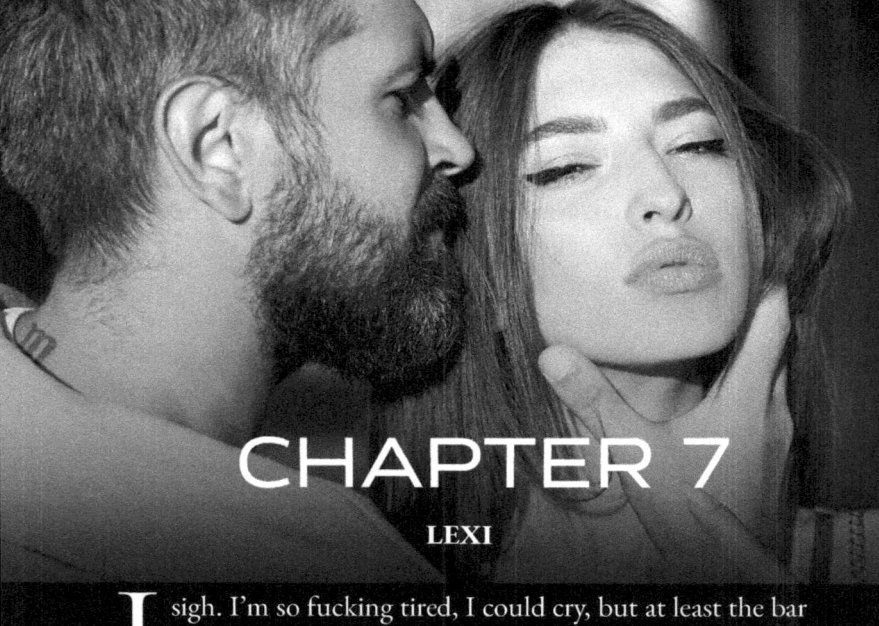

I sigh. I'm so fucking tired, I could cry, but at least the bar is empty, which means I can clean up and go to bed. My cut-off time is one a.m., but tonight, the brothers seemed rowdier than normal, and it took the girls hours to drag them off to bed.

I pop my earbuds in and find the nineties playlist on my phone. Britney Spears blasts into my ears, and I smile to myself as I grab a caddy and go to collect the glasses from the tables. I'm so lost humming and dancing that I don't see him until it's too late, and I crash hard against Axel. He stares down at me with curious eyes when I scream in fright, dropping the caddy and sending glasses splintering across the floor.

"Fuck," I mutter, removing my earbuds. "You made me jump." My eyes then fall to Grizz, who's propped up by Axel, clutching his side. There's blood oozing through his fingers, and the police officer in me jumps into action.

"He needs to lie flat," I say, rushing over to the couch. They follow, and Axel eases Grizz to lie down. He groans in pain, and his face goes a deathly white shade. I rip his shirt open and inspect the knife wound. It doesn't look too deep, and it's gone in at a fairly safe part of his abdomen. "He'll need this cleaned and stitched," I say, using his ripped shirt to press against the wound.

"Good observation, Florence Nightingale. What are you like at stitching?" asks Axel, going behind the bar and grabbing the first aid kit and some vodka.

"Me?"

He hands the vodka to Grizz, who unscrews the cap and gulps the liquid until at least half the bottle is gone. I stare wide-eyed, wondering how the hell he doesn't bring that right back up.

Axel unzips the first aid kit before taking the bottle back. He uses his fingers to part the wound, causing Grizz to groan. Then he tips the vodka right in there. I watch in disgust as the clear liquid mixes with the blood then splashes down his side and onto the couch. "Jesus fucking Christ," Grizz cries out.

"Don't be a big baby," Axel teases.

"Are you gonna patch me up or just stare?" Grizz snaps at me.

I crouch down to look in the first aid kit. There're all kinds of things here that usually only a paramedic or doctor would carry. I take out the needle and silk from a sterilized pouch. I've never stitched a wound before, but there's a first time for everything.

"What happened?" I ask as I kneel by his side. He's swigging from the bottle again as I carefully thread the needle and put on some gloves.

"You don't get the rundown, Mouse," says Axel.

"I just get the clean-up?" I ask, arching a brow. He walks away, ignoring me.

I take a deep breath and pierce the skin with the needle. Grizz winces and takes another swig. "How can you drink that stuff like it's water?"

"Easy when you're injured," he responds, glancing down to where I'm pinching his wound together.

"At least tell me the other guy didn't get away with nothing."

"He'll be dealt with," snaps Grizz, lying his head back and groaning as I pull the first stitch tight.

Axel adds, "By the police, of course."

"Yeah, of course," mutters Grizz. They couldn't make it sound less like a lie if they tried. Going to the police would raise too many questions, which is exactly why they haven't gone to the hospital.

Once I've patched Grizz up the best I can, Axel helps him to bed. I follow and watch from the doorway. "You gonna play nurse all night?" asks Grizz, winking. "I don't think I should be left alone."

"Do you think I should maybe stay and keep an eye on you?" I ask, laughing as he pushes out his bottom lip for extra sympathy.

He grins wider. "Yes," he answers at the same time Axel answers with a strong, "No."

I smirk, biting my lower lip. "Well, which is it?"

"Go to bed, Mouse," Axel orders.

I do a cheeky salute and head back downstairs to finish cleaning up.

It's another half-hour before I'm finally done. Getting the blood from the couch took longer than expected, plus I had the glasses to clean up that I'd dropped.

I pop my earbuds back in the case and frown when I hear a groaning noise. I move around the bar, listening harder. It comes again. "Hello?" I ask into thin air. It comes again, drawing my eyes to the floor. I'm confused, but when it comes a fourth time, I realise it's definitely coming from beneath me. I pull the large dusty rug back to find an opening, similar to a cellar door. Curiosity gets the best of me and I tug the door, but it doesn't budge.

Somehow, someone got underneath this building, and I've

been here all evening and not seen anyone use this door. I pull the rug back into place and head out into the carpark. I've never explored around the building, but as I move around to the side, I spot another door. It's also locked.

I decide to call Jack and pull out my mobile. He needs updating, and I don't often get a chance away from anyone to do it. He answers on the second ring. "About time. I was starting to worry," he mutters.

"Sorry, it's hard getting a minute."

"What yah got?"

"Not much. He's a hard one to crack, Jack. I don't know if he ever will. He came back tonight with Grizz, who had a stab wound."

"He say how it happened?"

"What do you think? The women are here for one thing and one thing only. But I have found a door to what I think is a cellar."

"Yeah, there is one on the blueprints I got. Have you been down there?"

"Not yet. It's locked. But I heard a noise from down there. It sounded like groaning."

"Go ask Axel."

I frown. "You think?"

"You're curious. What woman wouldn't be when they hear a noise?"

I nod, even though he can't see me. "Okay. I'll call when I have something."

I disconnect and head back inside. I take the stairs to Axel's room, which is at the end of the hall to all his brothers. I stop outside and raise a shaky hand, pausing before I knock. *What the fuck am I doing? He's going to yell if I go in there.* I sigh, knowing I don't have a choice.

I knock lightly. He doesn't answer, and I press my ear to the door, wondering if he's asleep already. Hearing the faint sound of running water, I realise he must be in the shower. I begin to think of a plan to get his key to the office, which is always on a small bunch he keeps in his pocket. If I can get into the office, I can get access to the key cabinet I saw when he was getting me the key for the bar's store cabinets. There're keys for each room in there.

I listen again. It's still running, so I carefully try the handle. I'm surprised when it opens, but I step inside, taking in the messed sheets on his bed. His room screams single male. There're clothes strewn over the floor, empty beer cans, and a half-drunk bottle of whiskey. I step over some items and spot his keys on the other side of the bed. I glance in the direction of the sound of him showering. I have to pass the bathroom, and the door is ajar.

With my heart hammering hard in my chest, I creep closer, peeking through the gap. His back is to me, and I sigh with relief, moving towards the goal, before a gust of wind blows the bathroom door. I hear it creak and instinctively turn in time to get a side profile view of Axel. His arm is resting against the shower wall, and his head is against his arm. His other hand is wrapped tightly around the biggest erection I've ever seen, and he's moving it so fast, I actually gasp aloud. His eyes shoot open, and he glares at me, his hand stilling but not releasing the chokehold he has on his cock.

"I just . . . I was just . . ." I trail off and run for the door, deciding I'm far too mortified to have been caught watching him than to try and think of a lie to cover my tracks.

I almost make it, pulling the door open as he slams a wet hand against it, closing it again. I freeze with my back to him and my eyes squeezed closed, praying to God to get me the fuck out of this.

"You like creeping around, watching men wank?" he growls in my ear. I shake my head, not trusting myself to speak. "You looked pretty turned-on back there, Mouse," he adds, and I feel his breath on my neck. The truth is, I've never seen a man touch himself like that, and I'd be lying if I said I wasn't excited right now. "I haven't been touched by a woman in a long time. Walking in here looking like you're wet through just for me is dangerous."

My breathing is rapid, and I squeeze my thighs together to ease the ache his words are causing there. This isn't part of the plan. *The plan.* I shake my head to clear the fog, but it doesn't work, and instead, I push back slightly, feeling his erection against my arse. I'm shocked at my own behaviour. It's like I've lost all control of my mind and I'm being completely controlled by my body. He's awoken something inside me that I didn't know was there.

He growls again, wrapping his arm around my shoulders and pulling me hard against his chest. "This is your last chance to get the fuck out of here, Mouse," he murmurs against my ear while pressing his cock against my arse and groaning. Even if I wanted to get out of here, my feet wouldn't take me, so I remain silent. "Don't say I didn't warn yah," he hisses, lifting me around the waist and carrying me over to the bed. He throws me onto it, and I let out a surprised scream. He doesn't even give me a chance to move my hair from my face before he's crawling over me, prowling like a panther until I fall back, feeling flustered and so fucking turned on.

As he moves up my body, his hands glide up my legs, over my hips, and up my waist, pushing my top up until my bra is revealed. He laughs. "Pink," he states. "Better." I find myself glowing under his praise, relieved I'd made the effort to wear better underwear since our last encounter.

He pushes my bra up over my breasts, dipping his head and sucking a nipple into his warm mouth. I close my eyes and groan as bursts of pleasure pulsate throughout my body. I grasp his shoulders as he moves to my other breast, paying it the same attention.

I'm aware of a sound, maybe the door opening, but I'm so lost in the feelings he's evoking from my body, I keep my eyes closed. He suddenly pulls away, and my eyes shoot open as he glances back over his shoulder. "Fuck," he mutters, climbing from me and dropping down next to me, throwing his arm over his eyes.

"Really, Ax?" Thalia leans against the doorframe, glaring at Axel. My face burns with embarrassment, and I tug my bra back down, followed by my top. "You booty call me, and I find you with a club whore?"

Humiliation drowns my sexual appetite away, and I feel sick with humiliation. He doesn't want me—he just wants sex. "Well, if you'd been here on time, I wouldn't have got distracted," he mutters, leaning up on his elbows. His erection stands proudly, and when he catches me looking, he grins. "Another time, Lex. I got business to attend to."

The way he dismisses me, like I am a club whore here for his needs, instantly wakes me up, and I scowl. "Yeah, this," I state, pushing to stand, "isn't happening again."

"Damn right, it isn't," snaps Thalia. "He's got a woman, bitch, so stay the fuck away from him."

"Really? That's not what he was telling me just now," I say, arching a brow. "Maybe train your dog and he won't stray." I storm from the room and rush up the next set of stairs to my own room. *Fuck, that was close.*

AXEL

I can't believe I lost control. It's like Lexi's got some voodoo magic on me, breaking every resolve I have. I pull on some shorts to cover my semi-hard erection, wondering if I'll ever get the fucker to deflate again. With images of Lexi practically begging me to fuck her just now, probably not.

"For the record, it wasn't a booty call," I tell Thalia. "I said it wasn't urgent."

"I was passing."

I glance at my watch. "At three in the morning? Who's looking after Zen?"

"Relax, it's taken care of." She moves farther into my room. "You didn't correct me," she says, smiling. "When I told her you had a woman."

"Cos maybe I have a woman," I say, picking up some of the shit from my floor and shoving it into the laundry basket. "Why the fuck did you warn her off me at the Zen relaunch?"

"Is that what you wanted to see me about?"

"The agreement was, I don't interfere with your personal life," I continue, "and I expect the same."

"Surely, you didn't call me here to tell me that?" She gently rakes her nails over my chest.

"You're right," I admit. "I called you here in the hope we'd fuck." She smiles wider, pushing up on her tiptoes to kiss me. I move my head, dodging her lips. "You're easy, and I needed a quick fix, but then I woke the fuck up and realised it was a mistake."

Her face morphs to anger. "Are you serious?"

"Deadly. Let's keep things professional. You run Zen, and I pretend you didn't fuck me over five years ago."

"If you're still not over that, why the hell did you get me back here to run Zen?"

"Because you're good at your job, and I need people who are good at their job."

"I'm good at other stuff too. Let me remind you." She plants her lips on mine, kissing me while her hand rubs my semi. I allow it for a few seconds before breaking the kiss and moving away from her wandering hands. If she'd have walked in before Lexi, I'd probably be fucking her hard right now, but since I've had a small taste of Lex, she's all I'm craving.

"No," I say firmly. "It's gone. The spark's not there. Just go."

"Jesus, you'd rather fuck that . . . that . . . cheap-looking whore than me?"

"She's part of my club, T. Leave her the fuck alone."

———

I manage a few hours' sleep where I mainly toss and turn and dream of all the shit I wanna change in this place. This club needs some serious money if I wanna keep it running, and to do that, I need the backing of the men.

I head down to breakfast, where Lexi is helping Duchess over by the stove. I take my seat at the head of the table. "Lexi," I say, "sit." I pull out the seat beside me.

"I'm busy," she responds, and even Duchess raises her brow in surprise.

"It wasn't a fucking polite request," I say, more firmly this time.

"I can manage," says Duchess, gently patting Lexi on the arm and nodding with reassurance. "Go do what he says."

Lexi rolls her eyes and slams her spatula down before making her way over. She sits a few seats down and fixes me with a hard stare. "What?"

"What?" I repeat, my voice dangerously low. "You got two seconds to readjust your attitude and move yourself to the seat I pulled out."

"That's not gonna work on me," she says, arching a brow.

I glance at Duchess to see if she's as shocked as I am. She's staring wide-eyed at Lexi, which confirms I'm hearing everything right. I stand, scraping the chair back. It takes me just one stride to reach her, and I pull her chair back effortlessly and scoop her up. "What the hell are you doing?" she yells, trying to get free.

I march towards my office, kicking the door open and letting it slam shut behind us. I dump her back on her feet. "How dare you disrespect me in my own fucking club?" I roar.

"You have to earn respect," she spits back.

"You don't think by letting you live here rent free that I'm showing you respect?"

"Don't throw that at me. I can pay rent, if that's what you want."

"I want to give an order in my own damn club and for you to follow it. Is this because of Thalia?"

She scowls. "Why would I give a shit about her?"

"So, it is about her. Look, that wasn't a booty call. I asked to see her when she was free, and that happened to be at three in the morning."

"What you do on your own time is up to you. You don't need to explain it to me." She turns, heading for the door, and panic takes over. I grab her arm and turn her to face me. I'm not ready for her to leave, especially when she thinks I'm fucking Thalia.

"There's nothing going on between me and T," I tell her.

She pulls free. "It's not my business," she repeats. "Besides, it's good she came in when she did."

"Oh, yeah, why's that?"

"Because I'm not the sort of girl you can use for a one-night stand."

"The only reason we stopped was cos she walked in, Mouse. That tells me you're exactly the sort of girl up for a one-night stand." I smirk, not seeing her hand until it collides with my cheek in a burning slap. I hiss in anger. "Motherfucker," I spit. She's got a good hand for such a small woman.

"Like I said, you want respect, you fucking earn it," she snaps, storming from the office.

It takes me a second to pull myself together before I give

chase, catching her at the door, about to leave. That alone sends fear through me. *I don't want her to go.* "I'm sorry," I blurt out, and she pauses with her hand resting on the door handle. "I shouldn't have said that." I sense some of my brothers watching. Maybe it's because they've never seen me apologise, as it's not the sort of thing I do. Or maybe because it's the first bit of woman drama I'm bringing to the club. But for once, I don't care. All I can think about is keeping her here.

She slowly turns to face me. "I'm sorry I slapped you," she whispers, staring down at her feet.

I step closer, brushing my hand against her cheek and running it into the hair at the base of her scalp. I gently tug until she's looking up at me, and then I kiss her. I'm not one for displaying affection, but her lips have been the only thing on my mind since the early hours of this morning. I pull her against me, ignoring the catcalls and whistles coming from our audience, lifting her until she wraps her legs around my waist, and then I carry her back to the office.

CHAPTER 8
LEXI

He doesn't break the kiss until he's kicked the office door closed and sits me on the edge of his desk. He stands between my legs and cups my jaw in both hands, staring down at me in amusement. "I'm too old for you," he whispers.

"We're two consenting adults." I don't know where this brazen woman has come from, but she's definitely causing me to make some stupid decisions.

Axel kisses me again, so hungry and desperate. The next thing I know, I'm reaching for the button of his jeans and pulling it open. He breaks the kiss, panting hard as he rests his forehead against my own and watches my hands pull the zipper down. He pushes his jeans halfway down his thighs and then waits for me to reach into his boxer shorts and wrap my hand around his lengthy erection. It's thick and solid in my hand, and he gasps as I trail my fingers along the shaft.

I don't want to break the moment, especially because I'm terrified he'll either laugh or run the hell away from me, but as I release his erection from his shorts, I say, "I'm not sure how to... erm—" He cuts me off with another toe-curling kiss and takes my hand in his, wrapping it around his cock and slowly moving it back and forth.

His free hand slides up my thighs, reaching under my denim skirt. He takes my knickers, pulling hard until the material gives way. He drags them from me triumphantly, holding them to his nose and inhaling. I feel my cheeks redden, not sure if I'm embarrassed by his hot actions or turned on.

He sits in the chair, causing my hand to fall away from his cock. He slides it closer, then takes my left leg, sliding a hand down until it's at the back of my knee, and gently lifts to place my foot on the arm of the chair. He then does the same with the right. For the first time, my legs are open in front of a man who isn't a medical professional, and I fight with myself to not ruin this by closing them and running out of here.

He presses a hand to my chest, and I lie back on the desk, staring at the ceiling. For a second, it reminds me of being in the doctor's examination chair. I smirk, but that idea soon evaporates when I feel his head between my thighs. Before I can protest, his tongue licks along my opening, and I cry out in surprise. He hooks his hands around my thighs, keeping my legs apart while he licks me again, this time slower, running his tongue over my sensitive clit and sucking against it. I feel more pressure as he uses his thumb to rub circles there as he dips his tongue inside me and hums his approval.

"Axel," I whisper, my words sounding breathy and desperate, "I've never had a man do this."

He pauses for a second but then dives right back in, like I've set him some kind of challenge. He licks and sucks like his life depends on it, and I feel a build-up begin in my toes, slowly burning a pathway up my body until it explodes. I cry out, surprising myself. I've only ever orgasmed by myself, and this is way more intense.

"That was fucking hot," he murmurs, standing to lean

over me and placing a chaste kiss on my lips. "But I gotta do something about this," he says, nodding down to his erection that's almost pressed against my opening.

He opens his desk drawer, reaching inside and producing a condom. I watch as he rips the packet, throwing it on the ground and then sliding the condom down his shaft. "You ready?" he asks, pressing the head of his cock at my entrance.

I nod, but nerves are pouring in and I'm beginning to realise the enormity of what I'm about to do. He must sense it because he pauses, looking back at my face. "Lex, I need words."

"It's just I . . . well, I haven't . . . so, I'm just really nervous."

"You haven't?" The head of his cock pushes against my opening again, and I wince. He frowns. "Lexi, you haven't what?"

"Done this," I admit. "I've never done this."

"Had a guy eat you out?"

I nod. "And have sex with me."

His frown deepens, and I realise he's only just getting it. "Wait, you've never fucked?"

I shake my head. "Nope."

He groans, staring down between us. "How?"

"Do we really need to discuss that now? Can't we just do it and then talk?" I fidget, hoping to slide him inside me, so I can get it over with.

He growls, stepping back. "Fuck, I feel like I'm back in school." His words sting, and I feel my cheeks burn with embarrassment. "Shit, sorry, that came out wrong."

I sit up, pushing my skirt back into place. "It's fine." I jump down off the desk, and he rushes to pin me against it by placing his arms either side of me.

"Lex, that's not how I meant it. It's just been a while since I heard that line is all."

"I should go and help with the breakfast clean-up," I mutter, keeping my eyes fixed on the ground.

He buries his nose into my hair and inhales. "How the fuck did you get to twenty-three untouched?"

"Simple. I avoided it."

"And now you're here, coming on my fucking desk." He groans again. "Jesus, Lex, I can't just fuck you like this."

I shrug. "It's fine, I get it."

"No, you don't. I'm not saying I don't want to."

"But you don't want to," I say, forcing a smile. "It's fine."

Axel grabs my hand and forces it against his erection. "Just knowing no one's been there makes me want to bend you over this desk and take it, trust me, but that's not right for you. I ain't the type of guy to lay you on a bed of roses and do that romantic shit, and for your first time, that's what you need. Christ, Lex, you waited this long to give it away, so don't waste it on me."

"What if I want to?" I whisper.

He shakes his head. "It's special. You're special. Give it to a man who means something." He steps back, freeing me from the confines of his desk. "Not a biker," he adds. "You won't find a special guy here who deserves you."

It takes me a good hour to pluck up the courage to call Jack. He answers on the second ring and sounds relieved to hear my voice. "How's it going?" he asks.

"Good, I think. Axel seems to be accepting me more." Images of his glistening mouth right after he made me come filter into my mind.

"You find anything yet?"

"Nope. The men are tight-lipped, and they only discuss business when they're in church behind closed doors. The women don't seem to know much either. It's hard to get anything from anyone."

"Have you tried getting closer to Axel or Grizz?"

"I'm trying," I say, feeling my cheeks burn at how close I actually got. "But they're hard men to crack. I'm not sure this is going to work, Jack."

"It's normal to feel like this, Lex. You're doing great. Just keep trying."

"How close am I supposed to get?"

He pauses before answering. "Has something happened?"

"No," I rush to say, "of course not. But these guys only get close to women they're fucking."

He laughs. "That's not true. You've got history in that club, so use it. Ask about your mum or the times you were there. Get Axel talking. He must remember stuff from back then."

"Okay, I'll try."

I feel deflated, and he must sense it because he adds, "Let's meet. Come to the flat tomorrow."

AXEL

Grizz slices open the pack of white powder and slides it closer to me for inspection. I lick my little finger, dip it in the coke, and rub it into my gum. I wait a few before nodding in approval. "Good stuff," I say as he cuts the second package and I test the next sample. I shake my head and point to the first. "We'll go with this one."

"Thank fuck cos I got a whole shipment coming in," says Rico, leaning over my desk to shake hands.

I wait for him to leave before turning to Grizz. "We move this shit quick. I don't want it hanging around."

The office door opens, and Lexi comes in backwards

carrying a tray. As she turns, her eyes run over the coke briefly before she looks at me. "Sorry, I thought you were in church," she says innocently. I adjust my trousers to accommodate the erection she immediately gives me.

"You're meant to knock," snaps Grizz.

"Like I said, I thought you were in church," she repeats, continuing into the room to change the drink decanters over. "What's all this?" she adds, nodding at the kilo packages. "Party for two?"

"You wanna join?" asks Grizz, hooking an arm around her waist and dancing against her while grinning. I watch as he nuzzles into her hair, and she giggles, her eyes briefly catching mine.

"Get the fuck off her," I snap. Anger pulsates from my head right down to my toes as Grizz continues to hold her. He grins at me, winking. "I'm not messing," I say, and his smile fades. He releases her, and she bites her lower lip, like she's trying not to laugh. "You better not be messing with this shit," I warn her, pointing at the cocaine. "Go do your fucking job and stay out my office unless I invite you in." I'm taking my jealousy out on her, and we both know it.

Grizz winces when she slams the door on her way out, then he turns to me and arches a brow. "You wanna explain what the fuck just happened?"

"Do you?" I snap.

"I was playing around with the barmaid."

"Yeah, well, this morning, she was laying on this fucking desk while I ate her pussy, so I don't appreciate you fucking around with her."

He stares at me for a silent minute. "You and her are a thing?"

"No, but that doesn't mean you and her can be."

He grins. "Brother, I didn't see that coming. I thought you said she was too young for you."

"She is," I mutter. "It was a moment of madness."

"Pres, you deserve a good woman, and I like Lexi. She'd have you on your toes, but she's a keeper."

"It ain't like that."

"You're warning brothers off her?" He laughs. "It's exactly like that."

"Get the fuck out and take this shit with you," I demand.

He laughs again, stacking the packages. "So, should I tell the brothers she's off the market?" That same anger reappears at the thought of my brothers touching Lexi.

"I'll tell them myself."

LEXI

Grizz smirks as he passes the bar, heading out. I find myself wondering if Axel told him everything, and then I begin to get paranoid, thinking they've been laughing at me. It's not like I intentionally decided to hold on to my virginity for any particular reason, but joining the police force was my top priority, and I never wanted a man to get in the way of that or steal my focus. It's not the type of job where you wanna go out on a Saturday night and drink with people you've probably arrested. And dating inside the force was not encouraged. Besides, who'd date another copper doing shift work? It would be impossible.

Axel takes a seat at the bar, and I place a glass down before him, filling it with his favourite whiskey. If I wasn't in role right now, I'd be pissed at how he spoke to me earlier, but as I've got to keep him on side—and obviously be professional—I force a smile. "Drugs," I say, placing the bottle back on the shelf. "Is that how you make money?"

"What about the ex?" he asks, picking up his glass and swirling the liquid around.

"He was from years ago. We're just friends now."

"You never had sex with him?"

"Nope. We were just kids."

"But he sniffs around you still. Doesn't he ever try it on?"

I smirk. "Not every man wants sex."

"Bullshit," he mutters. "Why did you split up?"

I shrug. "I don't remember. Like I said, we were young."

"A coincidence he's here and you grew up elsewhere, though."

I swallow down the panic. I wasn't prepared for question time right now. "Yeah. It's how we met again. I bumped into him in the hall of the flat when I moved in, and he recognised me. He's been here for years."

He looks sceptical. "And you had no idea?"

"Do you remember me being here when I was a kid?" I ask, changing the subject. I'm not prepared for the sadness that creeps into his eyes.

"Yes."

I'm surprised by his answer. "You must have only been . . ."

"Eighteen when you left," he states. "You were seven."

I nod. "What was I like?"

He smiles. "Quiet. Sad. Like a nervous little mouse."

Realising that's where my nickname comes from makes me smile. "I don't remember much," I almost whisper.

"Good. It's better that way."

"But I want to remember. I want to know what life was like then."

He shakes his head slowly. "No. No, you don't, Mouse. Leave it in the past where it belongs."

"You said before that your dad insisted Widow stay here with me, to keep me safe. Why? Why wasn't I safe away from here?"

"You just weren't, Lex," he says, sounding impatient this

time. "You know, I was thinking, maybe it's time you went home."

"To my flat?" I ask.

He shakes his head again. "Home to Nottingham."

My blood runs cold. I can't fuck this up now, and the thought of calling Jack and explaining makes me shudder. "No."

"You came here and saw Widow. What else is there for you here? She's not interested." He takes in my hurt expression and sighs. "She's too wrapped up in herself. She always was."

"I mean, I can't leave until I've paid back what I owe."

"So, tell me how much you owe and who it's to, and I'll sort it."

I frown. "You really want rid of me that badly?"

"It's just not the place for you, Mouse. You don't belong here."

"Funny, because I feel more at home here than I have anywhere," I lie. "This club feels like home."

He downs his drink and slams the glass on the bar. "Exactly the reason you should get out. I mean, what the fuck was your dad even thinking letting you come back here? I got you out," he snaps, running his fingers through his hair, "and now, you're back."

I let his words sink in before repeating them. "You got me out?"

He scowls. "Forget it, Lexi. Just leave." I watch as he stomps off in the direction of his office.

Shooter passes, and I throw my towel at him. "Can you watch the bar?" I ask. "I need to sort something." He begins to protest, telling me he's busy, but I ignore him and rush after Axel.

I don't bother knocking on the office door, which catches him by surprise. "What the fuck did that mean?" I demand to know.

"I shouldn't have said anything."

"But you did, so tell me, Axel. How did you get me out?"

He scrubs his hands over his face and groans. "Sit," he orders, and I do. "I was the one who called your dad. I tracked him down and told him where you were."

"Tracked him down?"

"He didn't see you back then. Your mum made things difficult for him."

"No," I say, frowning. "We all lived here in Manchester. She dumped us for her party lifestyle."

"He was a biker," says Axel. "Your dad."

I almost choke. "No. No, he wasn't."

"It's how they met. When she broke his heart, he went to Nottingham and joined their charter. It made shit easier for everyone cos when they were both here, it was like fire and fire."

"I don't remember him being a biker. Not even when I went to live with him." I mentally flick through all the jobs Dad had before finally settling as a lorry driver.

"He got out the life to give you a better one, and I don't fucking blame him. So, you can't be back here, Lexi. I can't be the reason you step back into it."

CHAPTER 9

AXEL

I wait for the brothers to file into church and settle down before I bang the gavel on the table. When I was a kid, that same sound made me jump. I'd be sitting on the floor, playing with my toy bikes while Dad and the men would talk around this exact table, in this exact room. I didn't realise the importance of it until I was older, maybe eight or nine, and even then, I never sat at the table. But my father thought it was important I learn the ropes very early on, and so I'd sit in the background, watching him, learning from him. *Fuck, I miss him.*

"We got shit to discuss," I begin. "Starting with Rico Narco."

Grizz slides the package we cut already into the centre of the table. "We got a lot of this shit to shift," he says with a grin.

"Are you fucking kidding me?" snaps Ice. "Tank will be turning in his grave."

I glare in his direction. "I don't have much of a choice, brother. I'm still cleaning up the shitstorm you caused."

He has the nerve to look pissed. "I was trying to stick to how your father ran things."

"And it got the club into a financial mess. You think it's

cheap running this place?" I snap. "You think the businesses are running so good, we can afford to relax? This is where the real money is."

"We had a deal with Matthews," he snaps. "It was working. He sold in our businesses, and it kept the punters coming back."

I laugh. "*You* had a deal. It ended when he stabbed our VP."

Ice frowns, pushing to stand. "Why are we only just hearing about this shit?"

"I'm telling you now," I yell, and he sits back down.

"And you don't think this is something we should vote on?" he argues.

"What do you think we're in here for, dickhead?" snaps Grizz.

"Where we gonna push this shit exactly?" asks Cash.

"We're not. Well, not directly. We're using Matthews's men. It's the exact same operation Matthews ran, but we're supplying, therefore, we're making the money."

"And what does Matthews say about all this?" asks Ice.

"You can go and ask him. He's in the lockup," I respond with a smirk. "You can deliver the news right before we end the fucker."

"End him?" he repeats. "When did we become this?"

"He stuck Grizz with a knife when we politely asked him to stay out of our premises. He threatened Thalia. The man's out of chances."

"You might be the President, but you don't just get to make the decisions," Ice snaps. "We take it to a vote like we always have."

"Fine," I say, standing. "All those in favour of the new business venture, say I." I patiently make my way around the table until I have everyone's approval. Everyone except Ice. "And those in favour of us ending Matthews for stabbing

Grizz and threatening Thalia, as well as dealing on our premises, say I." Again, I have a unanimous vote for yes, apart from Ice.

"Your vote against on both parts isn't enough to stop it, brother," Grizz tells him.

"Before we call it a day, I want to make it clear that no one is to make a move on Lexi." I avoid Grizz's snigger. "She won't be around for much longer, but until she goes home, she's off limits."

"You claiming her?" asks Ice.

I sigh heavily. "Your constant questioning is beginning to piss me off, Ice. I gave an order, follow it." I slam the gavel on the table and make my way out the room. I need air.

I break out into the car park and take some deep breaths. I'm lighting a cigarette when Lexi steps out, and when she sees me, she turns to go back inside. We haven't spoken since last night, when I asked her to leave. She took off to her room and this is the first time she's reappeared.

"All packed?" I ask, and she stops. "I can have your money by the end of the day."

"I don't need your money."

I take a drag on my cigarette, and she turns to face me again. "That's not true, is it? Who do you owe money to, Lexi?"

"I've paid it," she says, but I know by the look in her eyes that she's lying.

"Then there's no reason for you to stay."

"You don't get to order me out of here," she snaps. "I'll leave your clubhouse, but I'm not going back to Nottingham." She stomps back inside, slamming the door.

LEXI

I stuff the few clothes I brought with me into my rucksack. I'm dreading telling Jack, and I have no plan in place apart from sticking around the area and hoping I get another chance.

Heading downstairs, I run right into Ice, who's pacing angrily near the back door. We stare at each other, startled, and then he grabs my arm and pulls me out the door and across the yard until we're a few metres away from the building. "Where are you going?" he asks, pointing to my rucksack.

"I have a place," I say.

"So, why were you here?"

I glance back at the door. "What's all this about?"

"I don't understand why he brought you here, only to send you packing."

"He was helping me out, but I guess his good charity ran out."

Ice grunts, shaking his head and taking up pacing again. "He's making too many decisions. Maybe he's on the crack," he mutters, and I feel like he's talking more to himself than me.

"Cocaine?" I ask.

"He's happy to break my deals with Matthews and just run shit himself. It ain't easy," he snaps. "He thinks it's easy, but it ain't."

"Dealing?" I guess. He glances up, and I shrug. "I saw it on his desk."

He narrows his eyes. "He was snorting it?"

I shake my head. "I don't think so. He just had a large amount on the desk."

"And now, he wants me to go down there and tell Matthews that we're taking over. Fuck that. I can't take back my word."

"It's all a man's got," I say with a small smile. He glares at me harder, and I add, "My dad always says it."

"You know he warned us all off you?" he asks. He wipes his nose on his hand in a way that reminds me of a drug user, and I stare harder, trying to check his pupils. "What?" he snaps.

I shrug again. "You just seem . . . a little erratic."

"That's what he does to me," he snaps, pointing at the building behind me. "He's an ungrateful little prick. I ran shit, and he swans back here like he's the fucking king without a damn thank you. He makes his dickhead friend the Vice President, and me, I'm left to go clear the shit in the lockup, like I'm some little lap dog."

"The lockup?" I repeat.

"He's got Matthews there," he snaps. "Fuck knows how long he's been there. I bet he's pissed and shit himself. It'll fucking stink."

"He's in prison?" I ask innocently.

He laughs. "Allow me to show you," he mutters, grabbing my arm. I let him, mainly because I need to see what this lockup is all about and if it's something I can give to Jack.

Ice takes me to the side of the building where the locked door is. He pulls out a key, unlocking it, then nods for me to go inside. I take a look around before descending the stone steps. As I get to the bottom, a putrid smell hits me and I cough, placing a hand over my nose and mouth. "What is that?" I whisper.

"That's the smell of death," he mutters as we come to a stop at the bottom of the steps, where another door is bolted. He unlocks this one, and when it opens, the smell intensifies.

"Oh, Jesus," I hiss, pulling my shirt over my face. "That's disgusting."

He pulls a cord and light flickers on. I blink a few times before a man comes into view. He's tied to a table, spread out like Jesus on the cross, and he's very still. "Is he . . . is he dead?"

"I hope so," Ice mutters, moving close and shaking the

man's foot. He groans, and I sigh with relief. "Matthews, wake the fuck up."

"Ice?" croaks Matthews.

"What the fuck happened?"

"It got out of hand," he mutters.

"You can say that again. I can't get you out of this, man. You're gonna fucking die down here."

I begin to back out the room. I need to get Jack in on this and save this man's life before it's too late. I feel behind me, not taking my eyes off the men as I lift my foot to the step. Once I'm on it, I turn and rush up the stairs, breaking out into the open and gasping to fill my lungs with clean air.

I run towards the gate as Smoke steps from the gatehouse and eyes me suspiciously. "Let me out," I snap.

"I gotta clear it," he says.

"Are you joking?" I snap. "Axel kicked me out."

He shrugs and goes into the gatehouse to make the call. A minute later, he comes back out, just as the gate opens. "He cleared it," he says.

I nod and step through the gate. The fact Axel didn't bother to come out and say goodbye hurts me. And I have no business feeling this way.

———

Jack meets me at my old place. "You look tired," he notes as I shrug out of my jacket.

"You don't tend to sleep much when you're in a place waiting to be discovered. Did you know my dad was a biker?" I ask. The question throws him, and he stutters for an answer. "Great. What else aren't you telling me?"

"I thought you knew," he says.

"Bollocks. We don't have time for this right now. There's a

man tied up under the clubhouse. He's half-dead, and they plan on finishing the job."

"Who is it?"

"Does it matter?" I snap.

"Of course, it does, Lexi. Who is it?"

"A guy by the name Matthews. I think he's a dealer."

He gives a knowing nod. "Nick Matthews. We noticed he went off radar."

"Well, he's about to go off permanently if you don't go in there and get him out."

"I'll call it in but," he pauses, trying to find the right words before adding, "they might not want to blow your cover."

"Fuck that, Jack. A man's going to die, and we have to protect him."

"He's a nobody," he mutters cautiously, "and not worth throwing away this investigation." He goes into the kitchen to make the call.

I pull out my phone and there's a text message from Axel, which surprises me. He doesn't text, especially not me.

> Axel: Where are you?

> Me: Gone, like you ordered.

> Axel: I'm serious, Lex. I need to know where you are.

Jack comes in, and I stuff my phone in my back pocket. "I was right, they're not pulling you out."

"But they don't know I saw anything, only Ice and he was acting weird. I don't think it'll blow my cover."

"That's not good enough, Lexi. Matthews is a piece of shit. He deals drugs to vulnerable people and ruins lives. He's not our priority."

"But you could get the club on charges."

"For what? Kidnap, imprisoning? They won't stick and they won't break the club apart. We need more."

"Okay, well, there're drugs. They want to take over from Matthews and supply coke."

This gets Jack's interest. "How do you know?"

"I saw the coke."

"Where? Is there a lot?"

"I only saw a couple kilos, but Ice told me that's what they plan to do."

"We need more. Where it's stored, who's bringing it in, or how."

I nod before remembering my other news. I wince. "One small problem with that—he kicked me out."

AXEL

Ice groans, opening one bruised eye. "You're a fucking liability," I bark, punching him a fourth time. "You better pray she don't talk to anyone."

My phone bleeps, and I pull it out and stare at the message.

> Mouse: I'm with Edward right now, what's wrong?

I stare at the words until they blur. What the fuck is she doing with him? Images of her naked flick through my mind, and then I see him, removing her clothes, and I growl angrily, getting Grizz's attention. "Take over. I gotta deal with something."

> Me: Where the fuck are you, Lexi?

> Mouse: At my place. What's wrong?

I jump on my bike and spin away from the clubhouse, heading right for her flat. I pull up minutes later and jump off, anger spurring me on.

As I climb the steps to her building, another woman comes out, and I rush the last few steps to make it inside without buzzing. Maybe I'll catch them at it. The thought makes my palms itch for violence.

I bang on her door hard until she yanks it open. "What the hell?" she yells, and I shove her to one side and march right in.

"Where the hell is he?" I demand, pushing doors and opening cupboards. Lexi remains by the door with her hands on her hips, watching me in confusion. "Did you fuck him?" I realise I sound like a jealous arsehole, but I can't stop myself. The thought of her with someone else drives me crazy.

"You mean Edward?" she asks.

"Yeah, I mean fucking Edward. You run straight back into his arms, did you?"

"Well, you sent me away."

"Not so you could go back to him."

She slams her door, narrowing her eyes. "You told me to find a nice man, remember?"

My words haunt me, and I sigh. "Not him."

"He isn't a biker," she points out. "What are you even doing here?"

"Why didn't you just go straight back to Nottingham? Then maybe I would've stopped thinking about you," I yell then groan and give my head a shake. "You saw something you shouldn't have."

Realisation passes over her face. "You came here to shut me up?"

"I came to check you're okay."

"Fucking liar," she mutters.

"You know how it works, Mouse."

"Don't call me that," she snaps. "Your secret is safe with me. Don't worry."

"I want to take the risk, believe me, but I can't. Grizz knows, Ice knows, and if I let you walk away, they'll question my leadership."

"What exactly are you saying?" When I don't answer, her eyes widen. "Are you here to kill me?"

"No," I snap. "Not necessarily."

"That's reassuring."

"You'll have to come back to the clubhouse."

"So someone else can do it?" she screeches.

"No," I hiss again. "Where we can keep an eye on you."

"You kicked me out."

"I did. And now, I'm asking you to come back." Her expression is stubborn, and I sigh. "Look, just until my men see you're no threat to the club."

She snatches her unpacked bag from the couch. "Fine, but only because I'm not ready to die."

CHAPTER 10

LEXI

We get back to the club, and Axel follows me upstairs to my room. I'm nervous and struggling to hide it, but I fully expected to walk back into the place to a firing squad, or at least to be dragged back down to that hellhole they call the lockup.

"We'll pretend today never happened," he says, lingering in the doorway.

"Why is he even down there?" I ask, throwing my bag to the ground and pulling my jacket off.

"Club business."

"It was, until one of your men took me down there."

"I'm dealing with Ice, don't worry," he spits, looking disgusted.

"What's that supposed to mean?"

"Just keep your head down and stay away from the lockup."

"Because now you have two men down there? Fuck, Axel, aren't you worried you'll get caught?" And I realise I mean those words.

"Work the bar tonight. Ice was meant to, but . . ."

"But what?"

"I'm not gonna spill the club secrets to you, Lexi. You're not a part of it."

I scoff, grabbing my jacket. "Fine, I'll go then."

He blocks the doorway, confirming my suspicions that I won't be able to leave whenever I want. "Let's not make this an issue, Mouse. Forget about today."

"You warned your men off me?" I ask accusingly, changing tactics.

"I told you already, you're not gonna live this life. You won't be an old lady to anyone in my club."

"That's not your choice. You think you somehow rescued me all those years ago, and now, you have charge of what happens next?"

"Work the bar tonight." He walks out, slamming the door behind him.

I groan. He's so fucking locked down, I'll never get anything out of him. I pull off my top and shimmy out of my jeans. I need a shower to cool off and work out my next move. I'm just unhooking my bra when the door flies open. "And I actually did rescue you . . ." yells Axel, his sentence trailing off when he sees me. We stare at one another, and I see the heat in his eyes as they run the length of my body. I release the clip, but Axel quickly shakes his head. "Don't, Lex. Don't remove it."

I smirk, sliding the straps from my arms. "Scared you'll like what you see?" I drop it to the ground.

Axel kicks the door closed and takes a stride towards me. "What the fuck are you trying to do here?" His breathing is heavy and his eyes hooded.

"Why are you fighting this?" I ask, placing a hand on his chest. He stares down at it with apprehension. I stand on my tiptoes and run my hand up to his jaw. He doesn't make a move as I bring my lips closer to his. I tentatively kiss his mouth, once, twice, and on the third, I wrap my arms around his neck and pull him in for a deeper kiss. He allows it, letting his tongue slip between my lips. It ignites something inside me, and I push against him, forcing a more frantic, desperate kiss.

His hands slide into my hair, tugging it at the roots as he explores my mouth. He pulls my head back, exposing my neck, where he trails kisses. He moves down, nipping and licking my skin across my chest and down to my breast, where he takes my nipple into his mouth. Mini explosions erupt throughout my body, and when he releases it, I whimper in protest.

He takes my hand and presses it on the outside of his jeans, where his erection is bulging. "You feel that, Mouse?" I nod, lost in the heat of his eyes. "You feel what you do to me?"

"I wanna see," I whisper.

He groans, and it's a sound somewhere between pleasure and pain. He pops the button of his jeans and drops his hands to his sides. "Go for it."

I glance down at the bulge and swallow the nervous lump in my throat. I pull down the zipper, and Axel slides his jeans over his backside, to his thighs. He lowers into the chair by the window, keeping his eyes fixed on me.

I lower to my knees, settling between his legs, and I take his boxers and pull them down to reveal his enormous erection. "Oh." It slips out, and Axel laughs.

"You gonna touch it or just stare at it?"

"I'm not sure how," I admit. This is the closest I've ever been to a man's penis, which is ridiculous but there's no point lying to him. He'll know by my lack of skills.

His head falls back, and he moans. "You're killing me here, Mouse."

He takes my hand in his and guides me to his erection. "Wrap your hand around it." It feels warm and harder than I expected. He takes my other hand and also wraps that around. "Not so tight," he says, and I loosen my grip. He places his hand over the two of mine and begins to move up and down. "Slow at first," he instructs, then he takes his hand away, leaving me to take over. He relaxes, sliding lower in the chair with his eyes hooded and his breathing shallow. I continue to move my hands, checking his reaction to make sure I'm doing it right. "Move faster," he murmurs. I do, and he throws his head back, groaning.

Watching him makes me feel all kinds of ways and I fidget, trying to ease the ache between my legs. I bite my lower lip, thinking over my next move, but before I can talk myself out of it, I lick the tip of his cock. His eyes shoot open, and he stares at me wide-eyed. "Did I do it wrong?" I ask, feeling my confidence waver.

He shakes his head. "Do it again." This time, he watches as I lick the salty liquid dripping from the end of his cock. "Jesus, Mouse, you make me wanna come just watching your innocence."

I kneel up some more, removing one hand and using the other to guide him to my mouth. I wrap my lips around his length and slide him into my mouth until I gag, coughing violently until my eyes water. "Sorry," I squeeze out.

"No, it's all good. Try again, but maybe don't be so eager," he says with a smile.

I slide him in a second time, stopping before he hits the back of my throat. "Use your lips to cover your teeth," he says, stroking the side of my face, "then suck."

I do exactly what he says, sucking hard because he seems to react to that more. He runs his fingers through my hair, watching intently as I move my mouth up and down his shaft. Axel's skin glistens with sweat, and he balls his fists against his thighs. His panting becomes erratic. "Mouse, stop, I'm gonna —" He growls, stiffening, and then I feel the liquid hitting the back of my throat. It keeps coming until I have no choice but to swallow, and I almost gag at the bitter taste. Axel shudders, his fists finally uncurling as he relaxes his muscles. He strokes a hand along my hair, and I let his semi-hard cock slip from my mouth. "Sorry," he whispers, his eyes still closed and his head rested on the back of the chair. "You were too good."

I push to stand, desperate to rinse the taste of him from my mouth. Don't get me wrong, what we just did felt good and seeing him come apart right before my eyes was the hottest thing ever, but how do women do that shit over and over?

I make my way to the bathroom and fill a glass with water. I take a mouthful and swish before spitting it down the drain. Then I grab my toothbrush and brush my teeth until all I can taste is the minty freshness.

Axel is dressed when I go back into the room. He's almost at the door but stops when he feels my presence. "Sneaking off?" I ask, forcing a smile. I wish he'd already gone rather than me catch him sneaking out.

"I got shit to take care of," he mutters, avoiding my eyes.

"Okay." I turn my back, fussing with my backpack.

"Listen," he begins.

"Axel, it's fine. You don't owe me an explanation. We're good."

"You sure?"

"Catch you later," I say, sounding breezy.

AXEL

Whenever I'm around her, I do stupid shit. I say one thing and do another, and then she catches me leaving like some fucking rat. But I knew if I'd stayed in that room, I'd have fucked her. *Fucked her*, not made love like she deserves.

Grizz comes into the office and takes a seat. "You good, Pres?" he asks, and I nod. "Only you've been in here all night."

"I'm busy," I mutter.

"So busy, you can't join your men for a drink like you do every evening?"

"Yep."

"It looks like you're hiding."

"I ain't fucking hiding. From what?"

He shrugs. "I dunno. The fact we've beat Ice half to death and not told anyone?" He's right, it should've gone to the men for a vote, but my anger got the better of me when he announced Lexi saw Matthews in the lockup. Women never go down there, not even Duchess, and as Grizz keeps pointing out, we don't know Lexi, not really.

"I'm not hiding," I repeat. "I messed around with Lexi," I admit, "and now, I'm avoiding her."

He smirks. "That explains a lot."

"It does?"

"She's out there bouncing around like an energised bunny. I don't think I've seen her that happy."

I groan. "Don't fucking say that, Grizz."

"You don't want her to be happy?"

"Of course, I do. Just not here, not in this club."

"What's the deal with that? If you like her, what's holding you back?"

"She don't belong here. She was meant to have a better life."

"Come and have a drink with me. Forget Lexi and Ice. Just relax and forget your problems for an hour."

I nod, throwing down my pen. A drink does sound good.

We sit at the bar, and Grizz is right, Lexi is happier than normal. It only makes me feel worse. She places two glasses down before us and half fills them with whiskey. I expect her to speak to me, but she doesn't, instead moving back to Shadow, who she was talking to when we first sat down. "Maybe she isn't happy cos of you," Grizz says with a grin.

I roll my eyes and drink the whiskey in one. "Another," I

bark before she reaches Shadow. She sighs heavily so I can hear it, then she comes back to pour a second before doing the exact same thing. I narrow my eyes on Shadow, who shrugs at me helplessly.

"So, tell me what you do," I hear her ask him as she rests her elbows on the bar and gives him a bright smile.

"I just do as I'm told, lady," he answers in a gruff voice.

"Are you the beef they send if people don't do as they're told?" she asks in a teasing tone.

"Why you asking?" enquires Grizz, and she turns, resting her elbows behind her and fixing him with a flirty arched brow.

"I thought he might come sort me out," she says, grinning.

"You're not doing as you're told?" Grizz asks.

"I'm not sure. I'm quite good at following instructions, right, Pres?"

I feel Grizz and Shadow staring at me, waiting for a reaction. "Another," I order, holding up my now empty glass.

She sashays my way, grabbing the bottle and topping my glass. Before she pulls away, I grab her wrist. She wasn't expecting it, and she gasps, spilling whiskey over my hand and onto the bar. "You playing games, Mouse?" I growl close to her ear.

"Not as good as you," she says, her voice full of confidence.

"You've made your point. Put your fucking tits away and stop flirting with my men."

"Or?"

I grit my teeth in anger. I'm not used to being questioned, but this woman always finds something to throw back my way. "You don't know what you're playing with."

"Earlier, it was your cock," she says, smirking.

I growl, gripping her wrist tighter and pulling her half

across the bar. "You wanna play dangerous games with my men, Lexi?"

"Maybe."

I release her, practically shoving her back onto her side of the bar. She instantly rubs her wrist, and I see redness there. "Lexi's a virgin," I announce, and I hear her sharp intake of breath. "But she clearly wants to give that away to any fucker who'll take it, so have at it, boys. She's free to carry out your fantasies." I grab the bottle of whiskey and move away from the bar.

Duke stops me. "She's not off-limits?" he queries.

My body tenses, and I take a drink from the bottle to hide my anger at his question. "Nope. Forget what I said—she's free to fuck whoever she wants."

He grins, rubbing his hands together and moving to the bar. Fuck her. Once they've used her, I'll be over her. I slump down onto the couch and watch my brothers swarm around Lexi like flies on shit.

LEXI

My cheeks burn with embarrassment, still feeling numb and shocked by Axel's announcement. I was mad he'd practically ran out on me earlier, and now, he's acting like a prick.

I feel my phone vibrate and see Jack's name. "Smoke," I say, ignoring the men crowding the bar, "I gotta take this."

I step out, glancing around to check I'm alone before answering. "I was worried when I saw you left with him," he says before I can speak.

"It's all good. I'm back in."

"Thank fuck. Well done, Lexi. You got this."

Widow is coming through the gate as I disconnect. It's been a while since I last saw her, so I wait for her to get closer before saying hi. She looks up in surprise. "You're still here?" She doesn't sound pleased.

"Shouldn't I be?"

"I just don't understand why, when you have a place."

"But I got robbed, remember?"

She looks down at the floor again. "Doesn't mean they'll come back."

"I'm not taking the chance."

"Does your dad know you're here?"

"Speaking of him," I say, leaning against the wall. "He never told me he was a biker."

She shrugs. "So, ask him."

"I can't," I mutter. Asking him would alert him to everything going on here, and I know he'd be here before I could explain.

"Maybe you should go home and talk with him."

"Don't you want me around, Mum?" I ask, and she bristles at my words. "I thought you'd be pleased to see me and spend time getting to know me."

"I was never good enough for you, Lexi. Coming here to find me was a mistake." Her words hurt. I can't deny it. I never thought about actually feeling anything when I took this job. As far as I was concerned, she was nothing to me, not anymore. But now, I'm starting to wonder what else my dad kept from me. And I know it was out of love, but I'm curious. I want to know everything.

"You're right, you're not good enough for me," I snap, heading back inside.

CHAPTER 11

AXEL

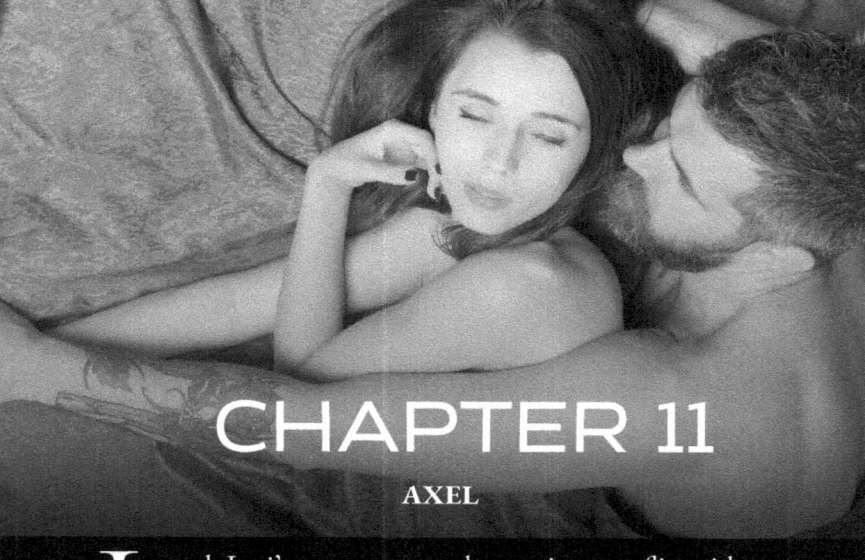

I watch Lexi's every move as she continues to flirt with any man in sight. And with each swig of the whiskey bottle, I grow more and more enraged.

I slam the bottle down and push to stand, swaying and grabbing onto the back of the couch to steady myself. She's by my side in a second, hooking her arm around my waist and wrapping mine over her shoulder. "Easy there," she says with a grin. "Let's get you to bed."

"I can walk," I mutter, but I don't bother to pull away because having her so close feels nice.

It takes a few minutes to climb the stairs to my room. I reach into my pocket and pull out my room key, which she takes to open the door. I stumble inside, pulling her with me. She lets me fall to the bed, where I stare at the ceiling. "Are you likely to be sick?" she asks as I feel her tugging my boot off, followed by the other.

"Do I look like the type of pussy who wastes good whiskey?"

"I don't think anyone means to be sick after drinking too much." She helps me to sit and tugs my kutte from me.

"Careful with that," I slur, and she places it gently on the back of the chair.

"Why do you all wear this?" she asks.

"Allegiance to the club," I murmur, closing my eyes. I feel her pulling at the button of my jeans, and I open one eye. "I don't think I'm capable," I say with a smirk.

She finally gets it open and pulls them down my thighs and off my legs. "You can't sleep in jeans," she says. "Widow told me to go home today."

"Yeah? Was she pissed you were flirting with my men too?"

She grabs one leg and shoves it onto the bed. I lift the other and slide up until my head hits the pillow. "I wasn't flirting. You openly announced I was a virgin."

I feel a stab of guilt. "I shouldn't have done that."

"That's not an apology," she says, arching a brow.

"I know."

"Sleep well," she says, shrugging.

I have the sudden urge to keep her here, so I grab her hand and she stops, looking down at our connection. I tug her gently, and she takes a step closer. "Lie with me?" I ask. When she makes no move, I add, "Please."

Lexi sighs and nods, so I shift over, and she lies down beside me, staring at the ceiling. "Tell me about my dad."

"Can't you ask him?"

She shakes her head. "No. He doesn't know I've come here looking for Widow. I don't want to upset him, so whatever you tell me, stays between us. I can't ask him about it."

I feel better knowing that because I'm not sure if Coop would want his daughter to know all about his past. "He was in our Nottingham charter, but he came here a lot. He got on well with Tank, my dad, and some of the other brothers from back in the day. He hooked up with Widow, and then she announced she was pregnant. Normally, if a club girl gets a biker like that, they're happy. They want to be someone's old lady, but not Widow. She was never mother material, which was why we were shocked when she said she was keeping you."

"Did she tell my dad right away?"

I shrug. "I dunno, but he came back often once he knew. Then she had you, and he came here for good, leaving Nottingham and joining our charter. But they argued all the time. It wasn't working, so he went back, leaving you here with your mum. She stayed away more and more from the club, occasionally coming back for a meal. You soon turned to skin and bone. I remember riding out with my dad once, and we stopped by your mum's place. You were there alone with no food or drink. Dad had enough and demanded she let you come back to the clubhouse. She soon started hanging with the guys again, but she didn't care where you were or if you could see what she was doing." I shake my head sadly. "I fucking hated that look in your eyes."

"Look?" she repeats.

I turn on my side, and she does the same. "So fucking sad, Mouse. You were so sad and quiet. The other kids ran around this place, but you, you just sat quiet. And then one night, I came back from a run, Dad was still out, and Widow was fucking a train of guys, one after the other. You were under the damn pool table with your eyes closed tight and your tiny hands over your ears, and she was on top fucking and sucking dick. It made me sick to my stomach. So, I called your dad, told him everything. He came that night and took you from your bed. I don't even think she noticed for a few days."

A tear rolls down her cheek, and I brush it with my thumb. "I knew your dad would take care of you. He left the club not long after. It's not often a man leaves or gets to walk away, but his pres saw the state you were in, and every time you heard the rumble of a bike, you'd get that same sad look on your face, so he let your dad walk. You were too traumatised for him to stay."

"You saved me," she whispers.

I smile, kissing her nose. "I told you I did."

"Which is why you don't want to see me back here?"

I nod. "Your dad loved you enough to leave this life. He wouldn't want you back here, and I respect that." She shifts closer until her head is on my arm. I pull her against my chest, kissing her hair gently. "Now, sleep," I tell her.

I wake with a dead arm and an aching erection. I open my eyes and take a second to appreciate the gorgeous woman in my arms. Her eyes flutter open, and she smiles when she sees me staring at her. "Morning," she whispers, turning in my arms so her back is to me. I wince as my cock pushes against her thigh, and she stiffens.

"Sorry," I mutter. She wriggles against me, causing me to hiss. "Mouse," I say with warning in my tone.

"If you're gonna keep me here, at least make it fun," she murmurs, letting her eyes drift closed.

I flop onto my back. "I've never had anyone in this bed all night," I muse.

"In *this* bed," she says, and I hear the smirk in her voice.

"I was in a relationship with Thalia, but she never stayed at the clubhouse."

"Why?"

I frown. "I'm not sure. She didn't really fit here. She wanted a bad boy, but she still had to maintain the image she was a good girl."

Lexi turns back to face me, lying on her side. "I've never had a serious boyfriend. I was so focussed . . ." She stops talking, gathers her words, and then continues. "On finding my mum and getting out of Nottingham."

"Really?"

"I remember some of the stuff about Mum," she admits. "The men, the sex, the tears she'd cry when they left her. And I grew up thinking all men would break my heart. I didn't want to cry for days like she did, and I didn't want to get used the way she was."

"So, you came to a biker club?" I ask, smirking.

She grins. "I always felt safe here. Here and with my dad."

I tuck her hair behind her ear and smile. "Which is exactly where you should've stayed, with your dad."

She hooks her leg over me and pushes to sit up. The second I feel her warmth pressing against my cock, it hardens again, straining to be inside her. "Mouse," I groan, throwing one arm over my eyes. She places her hands on my chest and slides against me. "Jesus, woman, are you trying to kill me?"

I open one eye, and she's smiling down at me with that cute expression she gets when she wants something. "I know you're probably going to break my heart." She rocks against me for a second time, and I grab her thighs, squeezing. Not being inside her is painful. "Or maybe, just maybe, I'll hurt you. But either way, why are we fighting something we both want?" She slips her top off, throwing it to the floor. My eyes are fixed on the pink lace bra, and she grins before also removing that.

"I don't deserve this," I mutter.

She takes my hands and guides them to her perfect breasts. "Just one time," she whispers, closing her eyes when I rub my thumbs over her nipples.

LEXI

I watch the conflict pass over his face. As if his mind is made up, he grabs me by the waist, turning us so I'm on the bed beneath him and he's over me like a prowling lion. Something about the predatory look in his eyes is hot.

He runs kisses across my chest and down to my breasts, taking his time to tease my nipples until I'm ready to combust. Then he continues down my body and settles his head between my legs. He uses his hands to keep my legs apart but spends so long just staring, I begin to feel self-conscious and try to clamp them shut. He holds them open. "I'm gonna take my time, Mouse. Don't rush me." I feel the warmth of his breath against me, and it sends shivers through my body. I just need him *there*. And as if he heard my prayers, he presses his tongue against me, sending flickers of pleasure right down to my toes.

He licks me, lapping at my opening like a starved animal, and when he slips a finger inside, I begin to see white spots at the back of my eyes. He keeps the pressure against my clit with his tongue, and I squirm against him, trying to get to the orgasm that's hanging on the edge. When I finally fall, it's with an earth-shattering explosion that has me crying out in pleasure while I grip my fingers into his hair.

He climbs back over my body, kissing me, and I can taste myself on his lips. He leans over and pulls open the bedside drawer, retrieving a condom. "You sure about this, Mouse?"

I nod. Nerves are beginning to build, but I shut them down. If I don't do this now, I'll be a virgin forever. I ignore the small voice in the back of my head warning me this is crossing a line, that this could ruin my case. If it gets out, everyone at the station will know. Jack will know. "Why do you look unsure?" he asks, breaking my racing thoughts.

I give a weak smile. "Just nervous."

He pulls the condom over his huge erection and places the empty packet on the side. "Do you wanna stop?"

"No."

He kisses me again, and I relax, wrapping my arms around

his neck. I feel his cock prodding at my entrance, but he keeps kissing me, distracting me as he slides in slowly. At first, it's not so bad, but the farther in he goes, the more uncomfortable I feel. He senses it and pauses to look down at me. "If you need me to stop, just say the words."

"Just do it," I say impatiently. I need this to be over with.

He braces himself on his hands and begins to move again, this time ignoring my wincing, and when a tear rolls down my cheek, he gently kisses it away. "You're doing great," he whispers against my temple.

I breathe a sigh of relief when he slides out of me. I'm sore already, and this is just the start. When he slides back in, it stings so bad, I have to turn my head away and squeeze my eyes closed. *Who the fuck does this for pleasure?*

"You okay?" he asks, and I nod, keeping my head to the side. "It gets better, I promise."

"When?" I ask, and he laughs against my neck.

"It's no consolation, but you feel fucking great to me."

"You're being way nicer than I expected," I whisper, turning back to face him.

He kisses me gently on the lips. "Don't expect it every time, Mouse. I'm the sort of guy to fuck . . . hard."

I'm not sure I like the sound of that, so I pull him in for more kisses to distract myself from the burning sensation between my legs. After a few minutes, he stiffens, groaning against my clammy skin, and then he stops moving, and I release the breath I'd been holding for the last minute at least.

Axel drops onto his stomach beside me and wraps his arms around the pillow. "We're gonna clean up, just give me a minute," he murmurs against the pillow.

"I can go and shower," I say, starting to sit up.

His arm dashes out, forcing me back down, and he tugs me closer. "In a minute, Mouse."

I lie beside him, staring at the ceiling. I just lost my virginity, and I feel like a weight's been lifted.

———

It's another twenty minutes before I hear his light snores. I carefully lift his arm and place it beside him before sliding from the bed. I look down and there's no blood, which I'm relieved about. The thought of him seeing that makes me shudder.

Dressing quickly, I creep to the door, carefully opening it and stepping out into the hallway. "Fancy seeing you here." It's Ice's cold voice, and I freeze, slowly turning to face him. "Good night?"

I take in his bruised, swollen face. "What happened?"

"What do you think happened, princess? Loverboy got all pissed because you ran. Why did you run?"

My mouth opens and closes a few times. "I was scared."

"Bullshit. I'm on to you."

He moves past me. "What do you mean?" I ask.

"Just watch your back, princess. I don't trust you, and I certainly don't think you're here for Widow."

I let him walk away before I rush up to my room. I take a few calming breaths then pick up my phone and call Jack.

"Ice doesn't trust me," I blurt out the minute he answers. "Right?"

"He basically just threatened me."

"Are you telling me you're compromised?"

"Yes . . . no . . . I don't fucking know."

"Take a breath, Lexi, and tell me what happened."

"He got beat up. He's a mess. I asked what happened, and he said Axel did it because I ran off yesterday. I said I ran because I was scared, and he didn't believe me. He said he's on to me and he doesn't trust me."

"He's got a bruised ego. It's an empty threat."

"What if it's not? What if he goes digging around?"

"He won't find anything. We've wiped your police record. You worked in a supermarket and a bar back home. That's it. That's all he can find."

"They know my dad. What if they contact him?"

"They won't. Besides, we're monitoring his phone lines."

I frown. "Since when?"

"Since you went in there. Any calls from the Chaos Demons will automatically be shut down."

"I'm getting worried."

"You're doing great. Just relax. Get something that'll close that club down, so we can both go home." He disconnects, and I throw my phone onto the bed.

"Easier said than done," I mutter out loud.

I jump in fright when a loud knock on the door scares the crap out of me. I jump away from it and let out a scream. "Lexi, open the door," shouts Axel.

Fear grips me at the thought he may have heard that conversation. I strip out of my clothes as quietly as possible. "I'm about to shower. Can I come and find you in a minute?" I ask.

"Open the fucking door," he growls.

My entire body begins to shake, and I contemplate calling Jack for help. "I'm naked," I say weakly.

"I'll kick it down if you don't open it right now."

I pace behind the door, shaking my hands like that'll somehow make this easier. I stop, take a deep breath, and plaster a smile on my face before sliding the lock. The door opens immediately, almost catching my foot. I jump back, and Axel glares at me, slamming the door closed. "You left."

"Huh?"

"I woke and you'd left."

"I was just going to take a shower."

He moves closer until he's standing right in front of me. He takes my face in his large hands and tips my head back to exam me. "Are you okay?"

"Yes." It comes out weak and sounding unsure.

"Did I upset you?" he asks, looking worried, and I shake my head. "Did I hurt you?" Tears build in the corners of my eyes and I panic. *Why the fuck am I crying?* He pulls me against his bare chest. "Fuck, Lex, I'm so sorry."

"No . . . it isn't you," I manage to squeak out. "I don't know what's wrong."

He pulls back to look at me again. "Maybe we shouldn't have—"

"No," I cut in, shaking my head. "We definitely should have. I'm glad we did."

"Tell your face that," he says with a small smile. "I fucked up."

"You didn't," I rush to correct him. "It was nice."

"Nice?" he repeats, laughing. "It was nice?"

I shrug helplessly. "It was terrible," I admit, and he laughs harder. "And I don't know why anyone would do that."

He pulls me against him again, and I feel his chest shake with laughter. "I swear, it gets better, Mouse. But we made a one-time deal, which means I don't get to see your pleasure." My heart twists, but he's right, it was a one-time deal.

I pull back, and he lets me, his arms falling to his sides. "I really need to shower."

"Mine's bigger," he says, pushing my bathroom door open and going inside. I hear the shower turn on and follow him.

"I meant alone."

"I ain't leaving you when you're all upset and shit," he says with a shrug. He shoves his boxers down his legs, and I arch a brow at his semi-hard erection. He gives a lopsided grin, and my heart swoons. "Worried you can't keep your hands off me?" he asks, stepping under the spray.

"I don't think I'll have any trouble," I say, removing my underwear.

The shower stall is small, and with him being overly large, I have to squeeze in. We take turns standing under the spray, and once I'm wet, he takes the soap and loads up my sponge. When he begins to wipe it over me, taking extra gentle care to clean between my legs, I can't help but smile. It's a soft side to him I've never seen until today . . . and I like it.

CHAPTER 12

AXEL

Once we're both showered and clean, I grab Lexi a towel and wrap her in it. She proceeds to brush her teeth while I dry off. I didn't bring any clothes with me, so I wrap the towel around my waist and go into her bedroom.

I wait on the bed while she does whatever she does in the bathroom, and when she appears, she smiles shyly. "Don't you have things to do?"

"Nope."

"But I'm fine, Axel. Honestly. I don't know why I got upset just then."

"You were overwhelmed," I say. "It was a lot."

She sits at her dressing table and opens a pot of something. "But I'm fine now. I promise."

I can't tell her I want to be with her today, that being around her makes me happy, so I just shrug. Tomorrow, I might feel different. I might not want to be anywhere near her, and I'll avoid her until she leaves. But right now, this is where I want to be.

I take her television remote and turn it on, scanning the channels while she applies various creams to her face. She watches me through the mirror. "I expected you to ignore me."

"What do you mean?" I know exactly what she means. She expected me to freak out and ignore her, and maybe I expected the same, but when I woke up and saw she was gone, I felt fear. I pictured her leaving the club, and it stirred all kinds of shit in my heart, shit I haven't felt since Thalia. It doesn't sit well with me, but I can't ignore it. The first thing I did when I saw she was gone was come to her room like a fucking hunter, and now, I don't wanna leave because I'm scared I hurt her in some way and the second I turn my back, she's gonna be out of here.

"You told me before you don't do romance, that I should find a guy who treats me right. So far, you're doing pretty good."

"Maybe so, Mouse, but I'll warn you, this might not last. I have a tendency to overthink, panic, and shut down." Honesty is better than pretending this is going places because who knows what my mind will decide tomorrow.

"I'll take it," she says with a small smile. "Even if it's temporary."

I settle on a black and white war film. "Are you feeling okay?" I ask, avoiding her eyes. "Like, down there?"

She laughs. "Yes, Axel, I'm fine."

"Good."

"Am I the first . . ." I glance over, and she's blushing. I love it when she does that. "Yah know, virgin?"

"You're the first twenty-three-year-old virgin I've met, let alone been with, but not the first virgin."

She turns on her stool to look at me. "Really? How many have there been?"

I arch a brow. "Altogether or just virgins?"

She thinks over my question. "Both."

"I have no idea how many in total. A lot. Virgins, two. Three including you."

"Oh." She stares down at her feet before adding. "Recently?"

"No, Mouse. Like I said, virgins are rare when you get to my age. When I was younger and discovering what sex was all about."

She stands and crawls on the bottom of the bed, facing me. She crosses her legs, which lifts her towel slightly. I smirk, and she tugs it back into place. "I'm still discovering, but I guess it can't be so bad if people do it over and over."

"It won't hurt so much next time. Haven't you ever experimented with guys?" I don't want to know the answer because I don't want to picture her with anyone else, but I can't believe she's lasted until now.

"Not really. Just kissing and stuff. I avoid dating, so the only men I've kissed were random strangers on a night out."

"And you were never tempted to take one home?"

She shakes her head. "Nope. I've never met anyone I liked enough." Her eyes are downcast again when she adds, "Until now."

"You shouldn't like me, Mouse. I'm no good for you."

"Have you had many serious relationships?"

I shake my head. "Just Thalia."

"Why did you break up?"

I stare at the television like I'm watching the film, but I'm thinking back to the day Thalia decided to end things. "I got sent to prison."

"She didn't want to wait for you?" she asks.

"Apparently not. It was five years. I didn't expect her to." It's a lie. I expected her to wait because, at one time, Thalia was the woman I wanted to marry. I guess all things happen for a reason. "What's your life like back in Nottingham?"

This brings a smile to her face. "I have a good life there. Friends, a nice place, my dad. I was always busy."

"And here?"

She shrugs. "It's not the same. I don't really have friends, only the sister of my best friend. My mum doesn't want to know me, which I kind of expected, but I thought it wouldn't bother me. Only it does. A lot."

I lean forward and take her under the arms, lifting her to sit over my knee. Her towel falls away, and when she tries to redo do it, I tap her hands until she gives up. "Maybe we can introduce you to some more people," I say, running my hands over her shoulders and down her arms. "We're throwing a charity thing this weekend. Loads of locals turn up."

"Okay. That sounds good."

I scoff. "It's a pain in my arse, but if I want to keep people on side, it's the best way."

"So, you throw parties for the locals just so they like you?" She smirks.

"No. So they don't complain when we're up to no good."

She arches a brow. "Um, and what sort of things do you do that they might want to report you for?"

I grin, wrapping her hair around my hand and tugging her lips to mine. "That's for me to know and you to find out."

The second time with Lexi was better, so much better. And technically, it wasn't supposed to happen, but we were naked and so close, it was a given. She didn't protest when I removed my towel and had her ride me at her own pace. Fuck, just thinking about it makes me hard. I adjust my shorts and open the fridge. I promised to feed her before I went for round three.

"Now, you're sleeping with the enemy?" I roll my eyes at the sound of Ice's voice.

"Grizz let you out then?" I ask as I grab some leftovers. I left it to Grizz because I was ready to kill the prick and that wasn't my decision to make alone. I guess the men voted to let him walk. *Pity*.

"I saw her coming out your room."

"I gotta clean up the mess you made, right?"

"So, you're sleeping with her to keep her sweet?" he asks.

"Exactly. And she's not the enemy. You are."

"I work hard for this club," he growls. "I made a deal with Matthews, and you went back on that. It was a shit move and it undermined me."

I slam the container of leftovers on the side. "Who the fuck are you talking to?" I get in his space, and he warily backs up to the wall. "I am the President, not you, so get that into your head before we really come to blows."

"You don't deserve it. Five years you were away, and it was me who helped Tank. Me who kept the club afloat."

"You made bad deals and almost ran it to the ground."

"Bullshit. I kept us clean, so we didn't end up inside like you. After you got sent down, the police were all over us. What do you think will happen when you start shifting Nico's drugs?"

"They're not watching us, brother. You're paranoid. They don't give a fuck about us because we're good at hiding what we do. Or we were until you let Lexi see the lockup. We can't afford to make mistakes like that."

"Don't you trust her?" he asks.

"I don't trust anyone. And because of you, I'm fucking her to keep her on side."

I catch movement by the door and know right away it's Lexi by the smirk on Ice's face. "Oops," he whispers.

"Fuck," I hiss, going after her.

I catch her around the waist right as she gets to the stairs. I pull her back against me while she fights to get free. "Calm the fuck down," I warn, dodging her head as she flails around. "That wasn't how it sounded."

"You fucking arsehole," she screams.

I glance back and notice some of the brothers watching our exchange. "Stop," I order her, and she stills. "You wanna talk, let's talk, but don't fucking run off or get all crazy." I bustle her into my office and slam the door. "I don't need my men seeing this bullshit," I snap.

She glares at me, her chest heaving. "Oh, I'm sorry, did I embarrass you?" she asks, her voice dripping with sarcasm.

"I was just saying that to Ice to shut him up. He fucked up, and I want him to realise that."

"By telling him you *have* to fuck me?"

"It's not how I meant it. We already had a thing," I snap.

"But today you had to seal the deal to keep me quiet? Well, guess what, Axel, I'm not going to run off and tell the police about the man you have in your basement because I don't want to be involved. And if you don't trust me, I'll stay here to put your mind at rest, but don't even think about coming near me again."

"I do trust you," I mutter, hating that she's pulling away from me when I'm not ready.

"I just heard what you said," she snaps. "I'm not some stupid club whore you can appease with bullshit. Keep away from me."

I watch as she storms out the office and heads upstairs. "*Fuck.*"

The following day, I call church. We have a shipment coming in on Saturday, which I've timed perfectly with the charity event. Half the local police force will be here to mingle with the locals, which means we'll have an hour's window where we'll be free to move our delivery from a truck to a shipping container in the scrap yard we rent.

We go over the plan several times, agreeing that Grizz and Duke will do the move. The rest of us will be here so we don't raise suspicion.

After church, I spot Widow at the bar and head over. She immediately smiles and places her hand against my chest in a suggestive manner. "What do you need, Pres?" I shudder, not just because she's way too old for me, but because I've fucked her daughter and I know that wouldn't be enough to put her off.

"I want you to stick around on Saturday."

"Oh yeah?" she asks, grinning wider.

"For Lexi," I say, rolling my eyes. Her hand drops to her side. "She came here to see you. Spend some time with her."

"I think we're a bit past that, Pres," she mutters.

I grab her chin hard and force her to look at me. "I don't care what you think, Widow. Your daughter came here to get to know her mother, and even though I agree with you and I think she's one hundred percent better off without you, it's what she wants. So, you'll be around on Saturday, and you'll make the fucking effort to be nice to her. Okay?" I release her, and she nods.

"Everything okay?" I look to the bar, where Lexi is watching us.

"Fine," I say, glaring at Widow, who offers a weak smile and a nod. "Widow was just telling me how she'll be around on Saturday for the charity event."

Lexi looks at her mum and smiles. "Great."

I take a seat at the bar as Widow scuttles off. Lexi gets me my usual without another word. She hasn't spoken to me since yesterday, and I hate it. "Are you okay?" I ask.

"Yes."

"You're not in pain?" I push because we did it twice and I knew she was already sore.

"Axel," she mutters, rolling her eyes.

"I just wanna check you're okay."

"I'm fine," she hisses. "You don't have to worry about me."

I drink the whiskey. "You know what I realised last night, Mouse?" She ignores me and continues to stack glasses. "That I sleep better with you next to me." When she still doesn't respond, I sigh. "I don't say it often, but I'm sorry."

"For saying what you said or that I heard it?" she snaps.

"For saying it. It was stupid. I was trying to be the man in front of Ice, but I didn't mean it. What we did yesterday was . . . special, and I'm glad you shared it with me."

"And then you ruined it."

I nod. "I did. I'm an idiot. I wish I could take it back, but I can't. So, I'm sorry. Like really fucking sorry."

A smile tugs at her lips. "You're not forgiven, but thanks."

I spend the rest of the evening at the bar watching her work. I take in every smile, every laugh. Savouring it, so when she leaves here, I'll at least have memories.

LEXI

Saturday comes and it's a hive of activity. Duchess is bossing all the girls around, giving us things to do.

I'm balancing precariously on a stool to hang a banner advertising the local kids' football team when I spot Thalia coming through the gates. Her white jeans cling to her long legs, and large sunglasses cover half her beautiful face. She's wearing heels and carrying a small, expensive-looking handbag, and I groan. "Why can't I look like that?" I ask, and Foxy looks up from where she's tying balloons.

"Thalia?" she asks.

"Yeah. She's so stunning."

"And a right bitch. It shows you can have all the looks, but if you're ugly on the inside, you'll never get the guy."

"You mean Axel?"

Foxy nods. "He's way too good for her."

"Really?" I laugh. "Didn't she dump him?"

"She waited until he was locked up and slowly pulled away. It sent him crazy being in there with no way of knowing what she was up to. One day, she'd visit, and the next, she wouldn't turn up. After everything he did for her."

"What did he do?" I ask, climbing down off the stool to admire my handiwork.

"She was the reason he went down."

"Really?"

"Yeah. He was saving her arse as usual. Not that she'd thank him for it. She loves to play the victim."

"He mentioned he'd been in prison but didn't say why."

"She was on a night out, even though he'd asked her not to go out alone. Anyway, she was flirting with some guy who got the wrong idea and tried it on with her. She freaked and called the Pres. Of course, he went running to help, it's the kind of guy he is." I think back to when I called him and he came right away when he hardly knew me. "He and Grizz found Thalia in the bathroom with this guy trying to kick the door in to get to her. She was terrified, and Axel naturally got mad. The guy refused to leave, so the Pres went nuts. He's got a temper."

"I can imagine," I mutter. His police report didn't read like that. It said a bar fight erupted because of Axel's jealousy. The man he assaulted ended up in hospital with broken ribs and a fractured jaw and eye socket, amongst other minor injuries. Grizz beat on one of the man's friends, and it was a similar story.

"He's a good man," she adds. "He deserves a good woman."

"I don't think he's looking for anyone," I say.

"He says that, but deep down, we all want someone. He just needs a woman who accepts him for him."

"And what is that exactly?"

"Everything that Axel does is for this club. He protects us, works hard for us, and he's there for us. He's a great President, and any woman who can come into this club and share his passion for it will be the woman of his dreams."

People began arriving an hour ago, and every time I look in Axel's direction, he's watching me. I was so angry when I overheard what he said to Ice, and if I wasn't here to do my job, I'd be a lot harder on him. But I can't lose my shit when none of this is for real. I sigh heavily. Everything is so messed up because I crossed a line. The worst thing is, I want this lie of a life so badly to be real, it's killing me.

His expression is full of anxiety, and I take pity on him and head over to where he's leaning against the clubhouse. "Everything okay?" I ask.

"Yep. You?"

I nod. "There's a lot of people here."

"I miss you," he blurts out.

I frown, confused by his words. "I haven't gone anywhere."

He takes me by the hand and pulls me inside the clubhouse. It's empty with everyone else outside. "I hate this distant thing you keep doing," he says. "Today is stressful enough having all the police turn up without you being cold and distant."

"Police?" I repeat.

"Yeah. They always come to anything like this. Shows community spirit."

My blood runs cold. *What if someone recognises me?* Not that I really met anyone from the station, but still. "I have to make a call," I say.

"Not until we're okay," he says.

I sigh. "Axel, we're good."

He cups my face. "You sure?" I nod, and he places a gentle kiss on my lips. "Thank you." It's so genuine that I smile. "I hate that I upset you." I didn't think he'd be bothered at all, and knowing he is makes my heart swell with happiness. "Go make your call and come find me."

I go to my room and lock the door before calling Jack. "What's up?"

"Are you still coming today?" I'd told him about the event, thinking it would be good to have two eyes on things. Plus, he's meant to be a part of the community.

"Yeah."

"Axel says the police will be here too."

"That's correct."

"Oh god, this isn't good. What if someone recognises me?"

"Like?"

"I don't know, Jack, anyone."

"No one knows you, and those who do, such as Commander Smithe, know the deal. Just act like you don't know anyone. I'll be there to make sure everything goes smoothly."

It's another hour before I spot Jack coming through the gates. Axel hasn't left my side since my phone call, so I interrupt his conversation with Ink. "My friend is here. I'll be right back." I slip from his arm and head over.

Jack embraces me like a long-lost friend, kissing my cheek and keeping his arm around my shoulders. "You okay?" he asks, and I nod. I haven't told him about the progress I've made with Axel, but now he's here, he's going to see it for himself.

"Actually, I need to talk to you."

"It can wait," Axel cuts in, grabbing my hand and pulling me away from Jack. I glance back helplessly and find him staring down at our joined hands,

Axel pulls me back inside the clubhouse. "What the fuck is he doing here?"

"Edward?" I ask innocently. "I thought everyone was welcome."

"Not your fucking ex-boyfriend," he snaps.

"Thalia's here," I point out.

"She works for me."

"He's just a friend. You don't have to worry about me and Ed, there's nothing like that between us."

"It didn't look like that from where I was standing."

I stand on my tiptoes and place a kiss on his lips. He relaxes. "You promised me some fun today."

He lifts me until my legs are wrapped around his waist. "I did."

The door opens and Thalia strides in. She spots us and narrows her eyes. "Are you serious?"

"Not now, T," mutters Axel.

"The barmaid?"

"As opposed to what," I ask, "the captain of the whore ship?" I hear Axel snigger.

Her face morphs to anger. "Are you going to let her talk to me like that?"

"You asked for that," says Axel, placing me back on my feet. He keeps hold of my hand and leads me back outside. I feel a sense of satisfaction that he's choosing me over her.

We mingle, and Axel introduces me to different people, including the local vicar and the head teacher of the primary school. He leaves me with them and goes off to take a call. When he returns, he's anxious again, looking around like he's waiting on something.

I wait until we're alone and squeeze his hand. "What's wrong?"

"Nothing." He stares back at the gate again. "Something. Grizz called, said there's a problem with a delivery and he might have to bring it here."

"Okay, so why the anxious face?"

"There are police here, Lex. Everywhere."

"Oh." My heart hammers in my chest. This could be it, the thing we need to end this mission of madness. I bite my lower lip. If it ends today, I'll never see Axel again. My heart twists painfully. "There must be somewhere else."

He shakes his head. "If he keeps driving round in circles while I try and sort something else, he'll ping too many ANPR cameras. That will alert the police and they'll pull him."

"And what will they find?" I ask cautiously. He's torn, I can see it in his face, so I add, "Look, maybe I can help, but I need to know what I'm dealing with here." He frowns, and I inwardly cringe at how much I sounded like a police officer. "Or not. Ignore me, I have no idea what to do."

"We need to get everyone out of here."

"A tour," I suggest, and his frown deepens. "Of the clubhouse. Offer everyone a tour. Or free drinks at the bar inside?"

He shakes his head. "It's too obvious."

"Just offer the tour," I say, more firmly this time. Before he can answer, I stand on a chair and clap to get everyone's attention. It's a lame attempt, and Smoke sees my struggle, so he puts his fingers in his mouth, whistling loud enough to get what I need.

I smile nervously. "What the fuck are you doing?" whispers Axel.

"Who wants a tour?" I ask, and everyone stares at me blankly. "Of the clubhouse," I add lamely. No one responds, but I smile wider. "Great, follow the President, Axel. He's gonna show you what that big old factory looks like these days."

"Me?" hisses Axel.

I jump down. "Yes. I can't. What if I show them something you don't want anyone to see? Besides, I don't know my way around fully." I watch as he stomps off to the entrance and sag with relief when everyone begins to trail after him.

Jack stops beside me. "You got a lot of explaining to do," he whispers. "And what's this all about?"

It's on the tip of my tongue to say the words that'll surely have this club shut down and Axel thrown back in prison. I wince before shrugging. "He wants to prove he's turning this place around."

Jack scowls. "But we know that isn't true."

"Okay," I whisper. "I think there's a big deal going down."

"What?" he growls. "Why am I only just hearing about this now?"

"Because I'm not sure if it's true, Jack. I told you he doesn't tell me anything, but I heard whispers about the market. An HGV is dropping off there now."

He glances at his watch. "Now? How the fuck am I gonna stop it with this short notice?"

"Don't you have someone out there?"

"What lorry? Where's it delivering to? There're about fifty stalls in that place."

I shrug again, and he groans. "I can't give you what I don't have. I only heard part of the conversation just now. He was on the phone."

Jack rushes off, shaking his head and pulling out his mobile phone. I head inside to join the back of the tour, but as I open the door, about six men rush out past me in the direction Jack went. I smile to myself.

Axel pushes through the small crowd. "That was weird. The police rushed out of here," he says, sounding relieved.

I glance around innocently, "Really? Maybe something's happened and they're needed."

He nods, kissing me on the head. "I have to call Grizz and give him the go-ahead. Smoke's taken over the tour."

I resist the urge to follow him. Seeing what he's up to will only make me feel guilty for not doing the right thing, so I force my feet to walk the tour as Smoke does his best to show the clubhouse off.

CHAPTER 13

AXEL

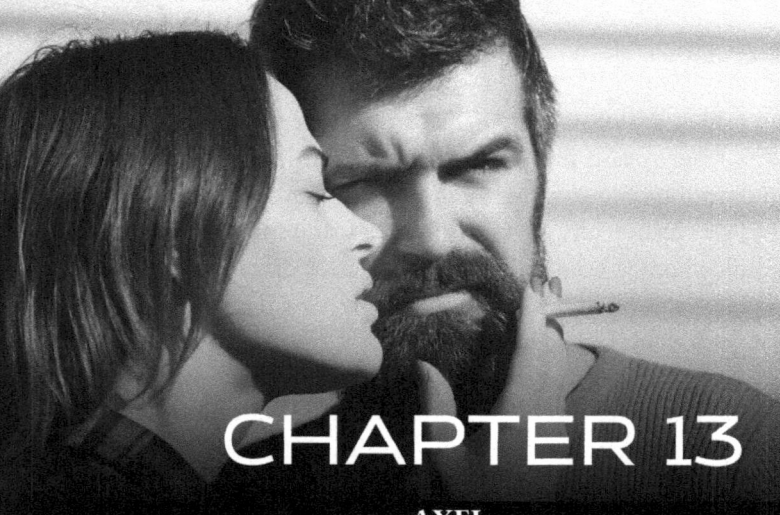

I relax the second Grizz turns off the engine and jumps out the van. It's well hidden out the back of the club, so the guys can unload it into the lockup until we can find somewhere else.

"What the hell happened?" I ask.

"There's a new security team on at the scrap yard, but they looked suspicious. I got a gut feeling, yah know?"

I nod, trusting his judgement. I'll call the owner and find out what's going down there. "Get this shit unloaded and get rid of this van."

As I'm walking back around to the front, Ice steps around the corner, blocking my path. "You claiming her or just fucking around?" he asks.

I sigh heavily, in no mood for his shit right now. "What's it gotta do with you?"

"I saw her looking cosy with a guy when you went off to tour strangers around our private clubhouse."

"We had a situation. I didn't have a choice."

"The guy looked pissed, and he ran off making a call. Not long after that, the cops ran out of here. Don't you think that's strange?"

I bristle at his words. "What are you saying?"

He shrugs. "Just making an observation, Pres."

I push past him and round the clubhouse. I find Lexi sitting on the wall, watching everyone. I've noticed she likes to sit back and watch. I rest against it and stare out into the crowd. "All sorted?" she asks, and I nod. "Good."

"Is your ex a copper?" I ask. I feel her tense and turn to her. "Fuck, Lex, is he?"

"No," she says quickly, "of course not."

"What were you talking to him about right before he left?"

"Nothing important. Why?"

Something about her posture isn't sitting well with me. "Let me be the judge of that. Tell me."

"He wanted to know if I was seeing anyone."

It instantly pisses me off. "And what did you tell him?"

"That I wasn't," she mutters.

I move to stand in front of her, resting my hands either side of her thighs. "You told me we were fine," I snap.

"I'm confused," she mumbles.

"I asked you earlier, and you said we were good, so why go and tell him you're not seeing anyone?" I'm aware I didn't make myself clear earlier, but she should have read between the lines.

"I didn't want to presume."

I cup her face with my hands. "I like having you around, Mouse. Way more than I should. And Ice broke his goddamn neck to tell me he saw you and your ex talking. I didn't like hearing that." My hand slides into her hair, and I gently tug her head back and kiss her.

"He doesn't like me," she says, and I pull back to look at her. "Since I left after he showed me the lockup, he's been a dick. He said I can't be trusted, that he'll ruin me."

"He threatened you and you didn't tell me?"

"I didn't think it was important. I have nothing to hide.

Let him think he's on to something," she says, shrugging. "Fuck him."

LEXI

Ice has been giving me dagger eyes all afternoon, and while Axel is busy lighting the fire pit, he makes his way over and sits beside me on the log. "There's something about you . . ."

"Here we go again," I mutter, looking unimpressed. "Did you hurt your neck running to tell Axel tales?"

He sniggers. "You looked pretty cosy is all I said."

"He's an old friend."

"Who dashed off seconds before the rest of the coppers ran out of here."

"So, it's a coincidence."

"I don't believe in coincidences. Like you turning up here out the blue and befriending our President."

"What is your problem?" I snap.

It gets Axel's attention, and he rushes over. "What's going on?"

"I told you already, Ice has some kind of problem with me," I snap, standing.

Grizz joins us. "Keep it down. There are still outsiders here."

"*She's* an outsider," snaps Ice. "Why aren't we questioning her?"

"About what?" I ask.

"Why you're here."

"She came to see Widow," snaps Axel. "Now, fuck off, because the way you're behaving is really pissing me off."

Ice shrugs before getting up and walking off. I stare after him, rattled that he's on to me. Axel breaks my thoughts by wrapping his arms around me. "Ignore him, Mouse. He's being a prick because I didn't make him VP. It's me he's trying to get at, not you."

"Why?"

He nuzzles into my neck, and Grizz walks off, leaving us alone. "Because he isn't fit for the job. I'm saving this club, and I can't do it with him beside me. You've seen how he is, suspicious of all the wrong people and doing deals with people like Matthews."

"The man in the lockup?"

"Not anymore," he says, kissing my neck.

I turn in his arms and stare up at him. "What happened to him?"

"Asking questions like this is gonna make people suspicious, Mouse. I know you're curious, but I ain't answering shit about this club."

"Earlier, when you were trying to think about a plan, I helped, right?"

He grins. "You let strangers in my clubhouse. Was that helping?"

I smile too. "It worked. Maybe I can help more. It must be hard dealing with everything by yourself."

"I'm not by myself, Lex. I have my brothers. Besides," he kisses me on the head, "if I let you in, you'll never be allowed to leave." He winks and wanders back off towards Grizz.

I take a walk away from everyone before pulling out my mobile to call Jack. When he answers, he sounds pissed. "Your intel was a pile of shit," he accuses.

"What?" I ask, trying to sound outraged.

"Six lorries were in that market, Lexi. Not one of them contained what we needed to end this club."

"Shit. Sorry, Jack. I really thought they said the market," I lie.

"Bullshit. Do I need to pull you out of there?"

"What? No, of course not." I feel my palms sweating and

my heart races. The thought of leaving the club, leaving Axel, makes me sick with anxiety.

"What was that today? He didn't leave your side."

"I'm doing what you sent me to do," I snap, glancing around to check I'm still alone. "You said get close."

"How close are you getting exactly?" I open my mouth to answer, but he adds, "Actually, don't fucking tell me because if it's how I think it is, I'll have to pull you and the entire operation goes to shit. You said you could do this, Lexi."

"I can." Guilt is eating away at me because, honestly, I'm torn. I wasn't expecting to feel loyalty to Axel, but today, when it came to it, I chose him, and that's never happened before. My job is my life. "I got it wrong today. I told you he plays his cards close to his chest. I'll do better."

"It's okay to get close, Lex," he says on a sigh. "Just make sure you can walk away after, because it will come to an end and that means you'll never be able to see him again."

"I've got this," I lie again.

All thoughts of telling him about Ice being on to me go to the back of my mind, and I end the call feeling a heavy weight on my shoulders.

I'm walking through the club to head up to bed. I'm shattered, and I have a lot of thinking to do. Mainly about how I'm going to get Jack the information he needs. Axel watches as I pass him sitting on the couch talking with Thalia. She's been hanging around all day like a bad fucking penny, giving me dog eyes and making snide comments, and I've ignored every single one because I'm not here for her.

"Lex," Axel calls out. I notice whenever he's around her, he doesn't use Mouse.

I stop and turn to him, smiling. "Yeah?"

"Where are you going? The night's just getting started."

"Leave her, Axel, she looks exhausted," says Thalia, gently squeezing his knee. "No woman likes bags that big under their eyes."

"Give it a rest, T," he mutters, getting up and coming over to me. He places his finger under my chin and lifts my head so I'm looking up at him. We stare at one another for a minute, and I begin to smile. He does this sometimes, stares so deeply, I feel like he can read my mind. And I have no idea what he's looking for when he stares so intently, but it makes me feel like the whole room fades away and it's just the two of us. Like we're connected so deeply, everything else disappears. "You can't go to bed without me," he says quietly.

"Then come."

"And leave these fuckers to party without supervision? Stay . . . please."

I groan. "Fine, but not for long."

He gives me a triumphant grin and leads me back to where he was sitting, pulling me into his lap and wrapping my hair around his hand. It's another thing I've noticed he likes to do when I'm close by.

"Ice seems to think you're not to be trusted," says Thalia.

"Not you as well," groans Axel. "Do I need to put a bullet in him to stop this shit?"

I lay a hand against his chest and smile, letting him know that I'm okay. Thalia scowls at where I touch him. "Maybe he's got a point," she adds.

"Thalia, you don't like me, I get it. But frankly, I don't give a shit. I don't have to justify myself to you or anyone else apart from Axel, and he's happy with my explanation. Don't you trust his judgement?"

Axel looks at her with a smirk and arches a brow, daring her to answer. She rolls her eyes and stands. "Whatever. Don't say you weren't warned."

I grin, turning in his lap to face him. "What did you see in her?" He watches her walk away, and I pull his face back to mine. "Apart from her body," I say with a laugh.

"I honestly don't know anymore." He cups my jaw and strokes his thumbs across my cheeks. "Your body is way better," he adds, kissing me.

"Flattery will get you everywhere."

Widow comes over, and I want to scream because I'm so sick of being interrupted. I'll never get to know him because there's always someone around. "Can we go for a chat?" she asks.

I frown, and Axel gives me a quick kiss on the cheek. "You stay here and talk. I've gotta speak to Grizz about business."

I slide from his lap and watch as he walks away. *Fuck, his arse looks great in those jeans.* "Now, that's a dreamy look right there," says Widow, sitting down.

"You're not drunk," I point out, because it's almost ten in the evening and she's never sober in the evenings.

"I've been wanting to talk all day, but you've been with Axel."

I look back over to where he is and admire the way his muscles bunch when he moves. "Yeah, we're getting on well."

"He's like that," she says, and I bring my attention back to her. "For the first few days, and then he'll get bored and pull away."

"Are you trying to warn me off him?" She's got nerve after not being in my life for so long.

"No. Just guard your heart. He's the kind of guy to stomp all over it."

"I'm a big girl."

"Doesn't mean it won't hurt."

"Is that what Dad did to you?" I ask. "Break your heart, or was it the other way around?"

"We weren't good for one another. We broke each other."

"I thought you left us."

"I guess Axel filled you in?"

I nod. "Did you miss me?"

She sighs. "I wasn't well back then. I'm still not, but I was worse. Your dad thought it was for the best, and I wasn't in a state to argue. He wouldn't let me see you until I was sober and away from the biker clubs. He hated my lifestyle."

"You chose it over us, though."

"I was selfish and a mess. And then I learned to live without you. I knew you were safe and well-loved. But, yes, I missed you."

"I thought you might want to see me now I'm older," I mutter.

"I do," she rushes to reassure me, and when I give her a doubtful expression, she shrugs. "It's hard seeing you. It reminds me of what I missed, and I promised your dad I'd keep you away from the club. He made a decision to leave and take care of you. He doesn't want you around this life. And now, I see you getting closer to Axel. Does your dad even know you're here yet?" I shake my head. "You have to tell him, Lexi."

Mum stays for another ten minutes, telling me about her life after I first left. Then, she gets called by one of the older members and scuttles off to do her thing. I notice Thalia buzzing around Axel again and head over to where there's a group of them talking. I jump onto Axel's back, and he immediately catches me so I can wrap my arms around his neck. I snuggle into him, inhaling the scent of his spicy aftershave. "I want to go to bed," I whisper.

He drags me around his body until I'm at his front. "Is that an invitation?" I nod, and he grins. "Let's go."

He carries me to his bedroom this time, throwing me on the bed and pouncing over me. I fall back, giggling like a schoolgirl, and realise I haven't felt this happy in a long time. It's a sobering thought, and Jack's words play on my mind.

"I can't get you out of my mind," he says against my stomach, where he's currently kissing as he pushes up my top.

I run my fingers through his hair. "Mum thinks you'll be bored in a few days."

"Like she knows me." He sits over me, staring down at my chest as he tugs my bra down, leaving it under my breasts. "She's wrong, though. There's something about you, Mouse." I know he's right because I feel it too. There's a pull that makes me want to give up everything just to have him close. "And I don't think I want to let you go."

"Same," I admit. "But we both know it can't last forever." Even as the words leave my mouth, they twist my heart.

"Why's that, Mouse?" he asks, leaning down and taking a nipple in his mouth. I sigh with pleasure, unable to form a reply while he's distracting me.

"You told me you don't do this, that it's just a bit of fun."

"Maybe I've changed my mind." He moves to my other nipple.

"I have a life in Nottingham," I remind him. He slides down my body, taking my jeans and underwear with him. I remove my top and bra completely then lie back, watching as he takes off his own clothes.

"Is it better than being here with me?" he asks, opening the drawer and taking out a condom. I shake my head, knowing it's not a lie. "Then we're settled, you're staying here."

I laugh. "I can't stay."

"Sure, you can, Mouse." He opens my legs. "I don't have the patience for foreplay right now. I need to be inside you." He settles between my legs and eases into me. I'm still sore from the other night, but he's right, it's not as bad as it was.

Axel begins to move, occasionally kissing me between thrusts. "You feel so fucking good, Mouse. I'm addicted."

"Fuck me like you would if I wasn't new to all this," I say.

He laughs. "No, it's too soon."

"I want to," I argue. "Please."

He slows his movements. "Lex, we have all the time in the world. We don't have to rush this."

"You said people enjoy it . . . show me."

He grins. "Aren't you enjoying this already?"

"I just want you to show me more."

AXEL

I lift her legs then push them down to her stomach, and as I move forward, she cries out. I instantly freeze. "Are you okay?" My size can make it uncomfortable for women, especially when they're inexperienced.

She nods. "That felt good," she says, her breathing coming out in shallow pants. "Keep going."

I start off slow, making sure she's comfortable before picking up the pace. Her cheeks turn pink, and her lips are swollen from our kisses. She looks fucking hot, and I have to squeeze my eyes closed and picture Grizz so I don't embarrass myself. It doesn't work, though, and I feel myself on the edge, so I pull out and step back, cursing under my breath. Lexi pushes herself onto her elbows. "Did I do something wrong?"

I shake my head. "The opposite. You're doing everything right, and I feel like a fucking teenager about to nut in two seconds."

She grins. "Can we change position?"

"Fuck, have you been reading up on this shit?" She rolls over, and I stare at her perfect arse. "Jesus, you're gonna kill me."

I stand behind her, gripping her hips as I slide into her wetness. She shudders as I watch my cock disappear into her and groan. Knowing I'm the only man to have been here just makes it more perfect. I like that she's mine, and my heart swells. I'm keeping her.

She lurches forward, and I have to hold her while she shakes through an orgasm. It's the first she's had from sex alone, and I smile as she cries in pleasure. "Holy shit," she gasps, pressing her face into the mattress. I continue to move, dragging every last shudder from her body, and when she finally sags in relief, I slam harder, chasing my own release.

She grabs fistfuls of the sheet as I slam into her. Tugging her hair, I grunt as I release into the condom. My legs are weak as I slide from her and remove the condom, taking it to the bathroom and disposing of it.

When I go back into the room, she's lying naked on the bed with her eyes closed. She looks stunning, and I stare for a minute before climbing over her and parting her legs. She groans in protest when I lick her entrance, tasting her pleasure dripping from her. It makes me semi-hard, and I slide up her body. "I just wanna feel you on me," I whisper, kissing her neck as I slide inside her. I moan against her cheek as she tightens around me. "You feel amazing," I whisper.

My cock hardens fully, and her eyes flutter open as I start to fuck her again. This time, I don't hold back, thrusting hard enough to move her up the bed. She grips my shoulders, gasping with each thrust. "Axel," she whispers. It comes out breathy, turning me on as it falls from her swollen lips.

I take her nipple between my fingers and tug it, sending her spiralling. She rakes her nails over my shoulder as her pussy squeezes my cock. I know I should pull out the second I feel it coming, but seeing her lose control while she cries my name is a new high, so I pump faster, squeezing her hip. "Axel," she whispers desperately, shoving at my chest. I ignore her, moving faster until I feel the first spurt of cum, and then I stop, letting the rest flow from me as I close my eyes and groan in pleasure.

I flop beside her, knowing that she's now glaring at me. I can feel the anger radiating from her. "What did you just do?"

"I know, sorry."

"Sorry?" she repeats like it's a curse word. "You're sorry?"

"I got lost in the moment," I mutter, opening one eye to find her angry face. "Don't be mad." I tug her down to kiss me, but she keeps her lips pressed together. I grin against her mouth. "I love a challenge," I mutter, cupping her breast and rolling her nipple. I hear her intake of breath and smile wider. "Don't make those noises, Mouse. I do stupid shit and make you mad."

"It's not funny," she snaps.

I nod. "I know. I'll take care of it tomorrow." I pull her to lie against my chest, knowing I have no intention of taking care of anything. If I can fill her with my babies, she'll stay.

CHAPTER 14

LEXI

I pace back and forth in the bathroom, cursing under my breath. I'm so fucking weak. Twice he fucked me bareback, and twice I let him. I groan, stopping in front of the mirror and staring at myself. I never thought about children. I wanted to get my career on track, and now, here I am, fucking it all up because of that sexy-arsed man in the bedroom. I had to lock the bathroom door to stop him following me in here and showering with me because I know it would have happened for a third time.

I get fully dressed before going back into the bedroom, where Axel is laying a tray full of breakfast items on the bed. He looks me up and down. "Going somewhere?"

"I should go the pharmacy," I mutter. I don't know why I feel like I shouldn't be open about this. He said he'd sort it today, but so far, he's made no mention of it.

"We can grab something after breakfast," he says, taking my hand and pulling me into his arms. "I made breakfast."

I smile at the tray of pastries and coffee. "Duchess made breakfast, you collected it," I say, and he grins, taking the hem of my shirt and pulling it from my body. "That's not a good idea," I say, trying to break free.

He laughs at my failed attempt, wrapping one arm around my waist and lifting me slightly off the floor while he unfastens my jeans and pushes them down my legs. "We can't dress before breakfast."

We sit opposite each other on the bed and tuck into the food. "Do you want kids?" I ask, then I blush because of our situation. "I mean in the future, not now, obviously."

"Yes," he says without thinking it over. "Do you?"

I shrug, and he eyes me. "I don't not want them," I say, "but I haven't thought about having them either."

"Mouse, we're having loads of kids, just so you know."

"What if I don't want any?"

He moves the tray to the floor and grabs me, pulling me to sit over him. "We're having babies."

"We only just started having sex," I say with a nervous laugh. "You don't even know me." And I want to die at how true that sentence is.

"When you came here, I wanted you," he says, unclipping my bra despite me trying to fight him off. "And I told you to walk away because I wasn't good enough for you." He throws my bra out of reach, and I groan. "But you stayed."

"We're not having sex again until I've been to the pharmacy," I warn, batting his wandering hands away.

"And then you tell me shit like you're all innocent, and I can't resist you. I'm a typical man . . . weak. And every time I kiss you, I hear this tiny voice telling me I shouldn't keep you here, you were meant to live a different life, get a good job and work hard, settle down and have kids. But there's something about you, and I can't give you up."

I let his words sink in, unsure how to respond because I want to agree so badly and tell him I feel exactly the same. Only there's a secret, one he can never find out. He grips my knickers in his hand and tugs once, snapping the material. I gasp. He does the same to the other side then pulls them away, throwing them on top of the bra. And I'm naked again. He's a fucking wizard.

"What are you saying, Axel?"

"That I'm keeping you, Mouse."

I'm so shocked, I don't even flinch as he lines himself up at my entrance and pulls me to sink onto him. He wants to keep me. He's offering forever.

"We don't know each other," I say lamely.

"We've got the rest of our lives to do that." When he realises I'm not going to move, he swaps us around so I'm underneath him. He slowly withdraws before sinking into me again. "Sometimes you just know, right?"

"You might change your mind. You even said yourself you might."

"Stop looking for excuses for why we won't work. We're doing this, Lex. I'm making the announcement today."

"Announcement?" I repeat.

"To the club," he says, lifting one of my legs and sinking in deep enough to make me cry out. "I have an old lady."

I stare at him in silence. I feel like I'm floating out of my body and looking down at this clusterfuck from above. He's saying everything my heart wants to hear, and my inner romantic is crying tears of joy, but the police officer in me is shaking her head and telling me I've made a huge mistake by coming here. Because when Axel finds out the truth, he'll kill me. Not only because I've lied but because I've made him look like a fool.

AXEL

I wanted to spend the day buried inside Lexi, but duty calls, and as I get into church, I feel a sense of pride that I'll be making my announcement. I laid awake for hours last night thinking of ways to not only make Lexi stay at the club with me, but also to settle the shit that Ice keeps spitting. Once she's mine officially, he'll have no choice but to keep it quiet because disrespecting an old lady is just as bad as disrespecting a brother.

Once everyone is settled, I sit back in my chair and let the smile spread over my face. It confuses the brothers, and I feel them shift uncomfortably. "Before I get to the clusterfuck that was yesterday, I have an announcement."

Cash grins. "Tell me it involves a free night at Zen."

"No, you already get a discount," I point out.

"He deserves a freebie, the amount he spends in there," says Grizz.

"Tell me you're not gonna claim her," Ice says with a groan.

I'm pissed he said the words before I could, and now, he's put a negative spin on it. I sigh heavily, fixing him with an expression that lets him know just how fucked-off I am with this bullshit. "I'm claiming Lexi."

There's not an immediate reaction. Some of the brothers wait to see if I'm kidding, but when I don't say anything, Grizz slaps me on the back and shakes my hand. "Nice one, Pres." The rest of the brothers follow his lead, but no one looks overly enthusiastic.

"Someone spit it out," I snap then glare back at Ice and add, "Not you."

"It just feels a bit soon, Pres, is all," says Duke. "But you know how you feel, and if Lexi is the one, we're happy for you."

"It doesn't feel like you are," I say.

"She's great," says Grizz, then he looks around the table. "And she's good for this place, right?" A few of the men nod.

"You told Thalia yet?" asks Ice.

"Why would I tell her?" I snap. "And why are you so concerned?"

He shrugs. "Just if you're done with her..."

I laugh. "What, you want a chance with the ice queen? She'll eat you alive."

"Not your problem now, though," he mutters.

"Let's move this shit along," Grizz cuts in. "Yesterday was a disaster, and now, we've got half a mill worth of coke in the building."

"Which we need rid of ASAP," I add. "If the feds get a whiff of this, we're all going down."

"We can't move it today. I got a call last night telling me the market was raided. The police turned up and checked every lorry and van on site. It might not be related, but we can't risk it," says Grizz.

"Get the women to move it," suggests Ink.

I think over his suggestion and glance at Grizz, who's looking as thoughtful as me. "It's an option," he says, shrugging. "A couple of kilos in shopping bags?"

"Where are we moving it to?" asks Shooter. "It can't be far if we're transporting on foot."

"There's a lockup two streets away," says Grizz. "I could hire one in another name?"

I shake my head. "We'd only end up moving it again in a few days."

"What about Lexi's flat?" Ice suggests. "Ain't it empty?"

I shake my head again. "I'm not involving her."

"Who's gonna look there?" he pushes.

"She got robbed, which is why she came here. Which reminds me, don't pull Widow in on this. She'll be too tempted to try and rob us."

"Zen?" asks Duke. "There's attic space."

I look to Grizz, who nods. "I'll go check it out."

After church, I go in search of Lexi. Her bedroom is

empty, and she isn't in mine because I locked it. I head back downstairs and ask Duchess, who's busy preparing dinner. "She went out," she tells me.

"Where?"

"I didn't ask," she says. "Was I supposed to?"

I shake my head and pull out my phone, calling her. When she doesn't answer, I open the app I put on both our phones last night while she was sleeping so I can locate her. I stare at the flashing dot telling me she's at the pharmacy down the road. I'd asked her to wait for me to sort it, and when I left her earlier, I asked her to stay inside the club.

I make it to the pharmacy before she's left, and I watch through the window as she steps out the consultation room. She thanks the woman behind her and makes her way to the exit, spotting me as she pulls the door. "Axel," she says, sounding surprised.

"Did you take it?" I ask.

She nods. "I didn't see the point in waiting for you when I can sort it myself."

"The point was I asked you to stay put," I say firmly, grabbing her hand and heading back to the clubhouse. I'm pissed she took the morning after pill, and I can't hide it.

"The good news is, I got the contraceptive pill," she says brightly.

I stop walking and turn to her, so she crashes against my chest. "Why?"

She frowns. "So, next time you get carried away, I won't have to come here. It was embarrassing being grilled in that room. She even asked if I'd had different partners in the last few days."

"You don't need to be on the pill," I snap, continuing to walk.

"It means you won't need condoms."

"We won't need any contraception, Mouse." We turn into the clubhouse car park. "Not condoms and not the pill. I'm claiming you."

"So?"

"So, the next step is babies."

She stops and lets go of my hand. "You're talking crazy," she says.

"I'm talking fucking sense," I snap, rounding on her and pushing my face into hers. "I asked you not to get the morning after pill."

"No, you didn't. You said you'd sort it, and I fucking knew you weren't going to bother."

"Lexi, filling you with my babies is top of my to-do list."

Her eyes widen. "We've only just started seeing each other."

"I've never claimed anyone before," I remind her. "This is a huge step for me."

"Stop," she yells. "Just stop. I never agreed to any of this, so stop telling me what comes next like I'm on board, because I'm not. I don't even know what it means when you say all that stuff."

I step to her, taking her hands in my own. "It means I love you, Lexi." She gasps. "It means I want to spend forever with you."

"You don't know me," she whispers.

"I know enough to know how I feel. I'm gonna go and see your dad next week and smooth it over with him."

She looks panicked. "No," she screeches. "You can't."

I cup her face in my hands and smile. "Mouse, this is happening. There ain't no way I'm letting you go. I waited five years to feel something, anything, and I set eyes on you and felt so much. I can't let you go even if I wanted to."

Tears fill her eyes. "You don't understand," she whispers. "I need to tell you—"

"What the fuck is he doing here?" I snap, looking past Lexi to the gate, where Edward stands.

She follows my line of sight and suddenly wipes her tears. "Oh shit."

"Let me get rid of him," I say, but she steps in front of me.

"Let me speak to him. It must be urgent for him to turn up here." I narrow my eyes in suspicion, but she rushes off to the gate, pushing out and walking off with him.

I stare after them until Grizz steps out. "You okay?" he asks.

"Something about him puts me on edge," I tell him.

"Who is it?"

"Lexi's 'friend'," I say, using air quotes. "They dated briefly and now they're friends. He just turned up here."

"You want me to have them followed?"

I shake my head. "I have to trust her. I can't make the same mistakes I made with Thalia."

LEXI

"You've ignored my calls," snaps Jack, marching at a pace I'm struggling to keep up with.

"It's been crazy these last few hours," I mutter.

"A shipment came in yesterday. Does the name Rico Narco mean anything?" I shake my head. It feels scrambled, and I'm having a hard time concentrating after Axel's weird behaviour, but I can't let it show after I reassured Jack I was doing good. "There was half a million pounds worth of drugs on that shipment."

I gasp. "Where is it now?"

"We lost it. It was followed off the boat, but someone removed the tracker. We found it at the docks."

I frown. I'm sure Axel would appear more stressed if he knew the police were tracking them. "He was acting odd yesterday, but he didn't say anything." I figure saying something is better than nothing. "Let me look around the club today and see if there's any clue."

"He wouldn't be stupid enough to have it at the club." Then he pauses. "Unless . . . unless that's what the diversion was." He glares at me. "Did you do it on purpose?"

I shake my head, my eyes wide with panic. "No."

He takes a second to process his thoughts. "What if he dropped the market on purpose to test you?"

"He wouldn't have," I say. "That would mean he knows about me, and he doesn't."

"How do you know?"

"Because he just announced to the club that he's taking me as his old lady."

Jack grabs me and pulls me down an alley, looking back to see if we're being followed. "Shit, Lex, what if he knows and this is all part of it?"

My heart slams heavy in my chest. "No. He doesn't know."

"How can you be sure?" he hisses.

"Because . . . I just had to take the morning after pill," I snap, and he glares at me. "He's talking the full shebang," I add. "Forever, kids."

He raises his eyebrows in surprise. "I'm pulling you out," he says, taking his mobile phone out.

I grab it off him. "No. Let me suss it out. If the drugs are at the clubhouse, I'll find them and call you."

He thinks over my words before reluctantly nodding. "Fine. I'll give you until midnight. If you don't find anything by then, meet me here. Either way, this ends today."

I nod, stepping from the alley and heading back to the clubhouse. I can't stop my tears as they flow freely. I'm not ready to give him up.

I don't get a chance to begin my search because the minute I step inside the clubhouse, I realise he's gathered everyone to make the announcement. He looks pissed, glaring at me as I enter and grabbing my hand. "All sorted?" I nod. "What did he want?"

"Erm . . ." I hadn't thought of an excuse because my head's too full of him and how I'm going to break his heart. "He was upset because of us," I lie. "He'd tried to call to talk about it and I didn't pick up."

"Have you been crying?"

"It was heated. He's upset."

"Did he fucking hurt you?" he demands.

I shake my head, but more tears slip down my cheeks and I swipe them away on my jumper sleeve. "No," I squeak out.

His expression softens and he leads me to his office. "Look, I know this seems a lot," he begins. "But in my world, it's normal. And I forget you're not used to that, so I'm sorry."

I smile through my tears. "That's at least the fourth apology you've given me."

He grins, wiping my wet cheeks with his hands. "I'll try and go slower if you try and speed up." I laugh. "This is a happy day. No tears." He kisses me until my toes curl and I'm breathless. "Let's go and announce it, so we can party."

Back in the main room are all the brothers as well as the club girls and some of the women from The Zen Den, including Thalia.

Axel keeps me at his side as he calls out to get everyone to be quiet, and as the noise dies down, he grins. "My brothers know this already, but just to bring everyone up to speed, I've got me an old lady." He holds up our conjoined hands and there're a few cheers around the room. Cali rushes over and throws her arms around me, followed by some of the other women. The men take turns kissing my cheeks and shaking hands with their President. It's a nice moment, and when Thalia approaches me, I prepare myself for her to ruin it. She leans close and air kisses my cheek.

"Good luck. You'll need it." She moves to Axel and places her hands on his cheeks, then she kisses him on the lips, lingering for longer than necessary. I roll my eyes in irritation. She wants a reaction, but I have too much going on right now to give it to her.

Mum embraces me, but there's a sad look in her eyes, and I'm not sure if she's sad for me or if it's because I might be sticking around.

Grizz whistles to get everyone's attention. "Now we have you all here, there's a job that needs doing. We need everyone but Widow and Duchess. You two can go about your business." He waits for them both to leave before continuing. "Ladies, we need you to transport some packages for us."

"You'll be leaving in pairs at hour intervals. You'll head straight to Zen, where Grizz will take the packages," Axel instructs. I'm mesmerised by him in President mode and find myself smiling.

"Are we allowed to ask what's in them?" asks Thalia.

"You can ask, but we won't answer," Axel responds with a wink.

"Do you still need me?" I whisper to him.

"Yeah, Mouse. Aren't you listening to Grizz?"

My heart slams hard in my chest. "You want me to take part too?"

"Of course. If I sit you out on this, Ice will have a field day."

I pull my hand free. "I don't care," I hiss. "I can't do this." Mainly because if this is what I think it is, I need to call Jack.

Axel backs me away from the others until I hit the wall. "Mouse, sometimes we have to get our hands dirty. And normally, I wouldn't have you anywhere near this, especially now you're my old lady. But we have something to prove to Ice and the other brothers who are doubting you. If you get stuck in with this, it'll earn their respect."

"I don't need their respect," I snap. "I don't give a shit about what they think."

He slams his hand to the left of my head, and I flinch. "Keep your voice down," he warns. "This isn't up for discussion, Lexi."

"Why can't you do it?" I ask, arching a brow, knowing full well he's not risking his own neck.

"In case the police are watching me."

"And what if they're watching the club as a whole?" I hiss.

"They're not going to suspect women carrying shopping bags."

I pinch the bridge of my nose, wanting to tell him how stupid he's being. "They'll see the pattern, Axel. Two women leave, fine, no problem. But then two more and two after that, all going to Zen? It's obvious."

"Lex," says Grizz, getting our attention, "you're up first with Thalia."

"Are you fucking shitting me?" I mutter. "Thalia, really?"

"Just do this for me, Mouse. You're first up, less risk."

"Unless I decide to behead your ex in the street," I snap, shoulder-barging him and marching over to where Grizz is holding out a Selfridges bag. I sigh, taking it and heading for the door, and Thalia follows.

I can't help but look around as we walk to Zen. There's no one obvious standing out, and I begin to relax. Grizz rides past us on his bike, not bothering to acknowledge us.

"I can't believe he's got you doing his dirty work," says Thalia, sniggering.

"Everyone needs to help out," I mutter.

"You're an old lady. You're supposed to live in a bubble of perfection, away from the shit."

"I'm not the kind of girl to sit back while everyone else does the work."

"As the President's old lady, that shouldn't be your choice."

I sigh heavily. "I know you don't like me, Thalia. I'm not thrilled about you either. But I'm with Axel, so either get over it or don't, I don't give a shit. But stop niggling in my ear like a little bitch. It's annoying."

I push the door and step into Zen, handing the bag right over to Grizz. My mobile rings and I spot Jack's name. "I have to take this," I mutter, stepping back out into the street.

"Don't speak," he tells me. "Just listen. We're raiding the clubhouse within the next half-hour. We're just getting suited up and waiting for the top to sign the paperwork. We know they're storing it there."

I instantly feel sick. "How?"

"The HGV was tracked on CCTV to a van. The van was tracked to the club and so on. I just thought I'd give you the heads up so you could get out of there if you can. But the officers going in know you're there, and they'll treat you like the rest until you get to the station so we don't blow your cover." He disconnects, and I get a fresh set of tears. *Fuck*. Now what?

CHAPTER 15

AXEL

I pace back and forth in the bar of the clubhouse until Lexi walks back through the door. I sag with relief and tug her towards me. She lets me, resting her head against my chest, but her arms drop to her sides. "Thank you," I whisper. "I promise that won't happen again."

"We need to talk," she mutters against my kutte.

I don't like the tone in her voice. Whatever she's about to say is going to upset me. "Can it wait?"

She shakes her head. "It's urgent." Dread fills my stomach as I lead her to the office. She closes the door and stares down at the ground. I have the sudden urge to create distance, so I move behind my desk and take a seat.

"I know you're pissed I sent you out there like that, but I explained—"

"You need to move the drugs."

"Drugs?" I repeat. I know she isn't stupid, but I've never said there were drugs here, and I certainly didn't tell her exactly what was in the package she just moved.

"We don't have time for this," she snaps. "Get them out of here now. And not to Zen either. Away from anything that is Chaos Demons."

"Why?" I ask, feeling tense.

"Because you're about to be raided by the police."

All kinds of questions run through my head as I stare at her guilt-ridden face. But right now, I don't have time to analyse it, so I dive up out my chair and rush back into the main room, yelling, "We need the packages out here now! Ladies, keep your bag, jump on the back of a bike. Brothers, take them to where Matthews is." It's a code only my brothers will know because right now, they're all I can trust.

Everyone begins to move, reacting to the urgency in my voice. I put a call in to Grizz and tell him the plan. He agrees to take the packages he has already to the meeting point.

Lexi steps out the office. "Is there anything else here?" she asks. "Because they'll have a warrant to search everywhere."

I stiffen at the sound of her voice. "How do you know all this?"

"I know someone in the force."

"Edward?" I guess, and she doesn't reply. "Fuck, Lexi, you've got some explaining to do."

It's almost ten minutes later when we hear car doors slamming. I made sure to leave the gates of the club open, so they didn't damage them busting in here. Lexi stands behind the bar as I open the door with a smile. "Good evening," I greet, opening wider so they can file in. The officer at front gives the usual spiel about having a warrant to search the premises. I'm told to take a seat while they begin to make their way through the clubhouse. Lexi is made to sit beside me.

"I'm going to ask you a question, Lexi, and I need the truth," I murmur. I can see she's nervous by the way she twists her fingers together. "Have you been feeding information back to Edward?"

She shakes her head. "No."

"So, how did they know?"

"I'm not sure. I heard about the raid and came straight here."

The officer watching over us moves Lexi to the other side of the room, so we can't talk.

It's an hour before the main officer is back before me, handing over a copy of the search warrant. "For your records," he says coldly.

"Thanks. Did you find what you were looking for?"

He scoffs. "Wouldn't you have been arrested if I did?"

I follow them to the door, closing it behind the last one. "I don't even know where to begin," I say, turning to Lexi.

"At least they didn't find anything."

"It was close, Lexi. Way too close. How the fuck did they know it was here?" Something is off, and she's not quite meeting my eyes.

Grizz comes in, followed by some of the others. He pats me on the back. "That was close, Pres."

"Too close," Duke agrees. "How did you find out about the raid?"

I nod towards Lexi. "Her ex is a police officer."

"That could come in handy," says Smoke.

"You sure you've got all the facts, Pres?" asks Ice, moving to where I stand and turning to look at Lexi. "Cos I just got off the phone from her old man, and he told me she's the copper."

LEXI

The room is deathly quiet, and all eyes are now on me. I stopped breathing the second Ice began that sentence. "He reckons she took some good job in Manchester," he continues.

"Lexi?" asks Axel, and his voice cracks slightly, like he's unsure where this is going to go.

"Everyone clear out," yells Grizz. Everyone passes me, all heading upstairs until there's just me, Axel, Grizz, and Ice left. "You need to start talking, Lex," he demands.

"I tried to tell you," I begin. It was the wrong thing to say, and I slam my mouth closed when Axel lets out a roar so aggressive, I flinch and squeeze my eyes closed. When I next open them, he's moving towards me with a gun in his hand, and all I can think is, *where did he get that when the police just searched him?*

I back up until my legs hit a table. "Tell me he's lying," he growls, pushing the gun against my temple. I wince as the cold metal cools my clammy skin. "Tell me he's fucking lying."

I stay quiet, figuring my words will only anger him more, and with a gun to my head, that's the last thing I want to do. All my training for this kind of situation disappears, and I'm left feeling terrified. "Are you a bastard copper?" he yells, pressing the gun harder.

"Yes," I mutter, closing my eyes and waiting for the sound of his gun releasing a bullet.

I feel him step away, taking the gun with him, and when I open my eyes, his back is to me and he's bent over, resting his hands on his knees and taking deep, painful-sounding breaths. "Get her out of here," he mutters between heavy heaves. Ice comes towards me, but Axel holds up a hand. "Not you," he growls. "Grizz."

Grizz makes no eye contact as he grabs my upper arm and pulls me behind him towards the door. He drags me around to the back of the clubhouse until we get to the door that leads down to the basement.

Once inside, he shoves me into the middle of the room. "Undress," he orders. He's checking for wires, so I remove my shirt and slowly turn, showing him I have nothing. He grabs my shirt and checks it. "And the rest," he snaps. I slide out of my jeans and kick them to him, where he checks them before throwing my clothes in a pile. "Phone?" he asks.

I remove it from my bra, and he arches a brow before taking it and opening the back. When he's satisfied, he orders me to sit on the stool. He grabs handcuffs from a cupboard and cuffs my hands together. "Do you check in?" I don't reply, and he holds up my phone. "I'll check anyway, so you may as well tell me."

"Just as long as I make contact every day. But he'll expect to hear from me soon after they didn't find anything here."

He leaves, slamming the door closed and locking it.

I sag in relief and let the tears fall freely. It's like a weight's been lifted because now Axel knows the truth. But there's also a feeling of sickness and dread, knowing he'll hate me forever.

AXEL

I can't shake the feeling of total disappointment mixed with anger and hatred. The questions run over and over in my mind as I watch her sleep in the corner of the lockup. I've never felt so fucking betrayed, and it's eating away at my soul. She occasionally flinches, and I wonder if she's dreaming about me ending her life.

I need to be in church in ten minutes and I came down here an hour ago with the intention of getting some answers, but she was already curled up in the corner sleeping, so I found myself just watching, trying to turn my love into hatred.

She suddenly sits up and looks around dazed. When she sees me watching her, she drags her knees to her chest and stares back with mistrusting eyes. I want to laugh at her audacity.

"Why?" I ask.

"It's my job," she whispers. Her voice is croaky from lack of water, and by the looks of her swollen eyes, too many tears.

"I mean, why did you make it so personal?"

"It just happened."

"Because I was so easy, right?" I snap, running my fingers through my hair for the hundredth time. "Such a fucking pushover."

"No," she whispers, and I think I see the glistening of more tears.

"Don't you dare fucking cry," I yell. "You realise you chose the wrong target to cosy up to? Ice would've spilled his guts the second he got a sniff of that virgin pussy and told you all the secrets." I scoff. "Was you even a virgin?" I remember looking at the sheets and seeing no sign of blood.

"Yes," she mutters.

"You let me think we had something," I yell. "I defended you to my men."

"I'm sorry."

"Ice told me to watch my back, and I ignored him. I look like a fucking idiot!" I shout then take a calming breath. "Sorry isn't enough. Not even close. You've betrayed me and made me look a fool."

I leave because staying would only make me end her a lot sooner than I should. We've got to figure a way to resolve this and soon.

The men are silent when I enter church. I've betrayed them, and they feel it. I can see it in their eyes. Ice looks smug, and I wonder if taking my anger out on his face will ease the urge any.

I bang the gavel on the table and sit down. "I fucked up," I begin. "I took my eye off the ball."

"We all did," says Grizz.

"Except me," Ice cuts in.

"I should've listened," I admit to him, even though it kills me. "At least heard you out."

"There's no point going over it," says Smoke. "We have to figure out what to do."

"Have you spoken to her?" Grizz asks.

I shake my head. "Not properly. I can't be around her without wanting to choke the fucking life out of her."

"I know you're not gonna like this, but she's gotta call her handler," Grizz tells me. "If she doesn't check in soon, he's gonna wonder what the fuck's happening."

"Can I just point out that she told you, and that's gotta count for something," says Smoke sheepishly. The other men glare at him, and he shrugs. "I'm just saying, she saved our arses when it came down to it."

"Our arses wouldn't have been in that situation had she not infiltrated our club," snaps Ice. "We gotta end her and show others we're not gonna take shit lying down."

"The real question is," I mutter, feeling my heart slamming hard in my chest, "do you still want me as your President?" The air turns cold as I glance at each of my men individually. "We gotta vote on it," I stand, "but without me present." I hand the gavel to Grizz.

"Pres, come on, let's not do this now," he says.

"I can't lead this club if there's no confidence in me. Take the vote," I order, walking out.

Leaning against the wall opposite church, I rest my head back and stare at the ceiling. I've never thought about what I'd do if I don't keep my presidency at the club. Maybe I'd go nomad for a while. I like the sound of being totally free of everything.

Grizz opens the door, disrupting my thoughts. I go back inside, and Grizz points to my chair. "Take a seat, Pres," he says with a wink, and relief floods me. The fact they can forgive for something so fucking huge, something that could've brought the club down, means a lot. I sit and notice Ice's face is stone. I don't blame him for voting against me—I would have.

"We gotta get her out of the lockup," says Grizz. "She ain't going anywhere cos we have something on her. Not only did she run drugs for the club, she also fed us information, which gets her up on a charge of perverting the course of justice at least. But she needs to be with a brother at all times."

I nod in agreement. "But not me," I say.

"You don't think you have to take a fucking turn babysitting this bitch?" snaps Ice. "She's your old lady." My blood turns cold again. *My old lady. Fuck.*

"Maybe he's got a point. She's more likely to open up to you than anyone, and if the police have anything else on us, we need to know," says Duke.

I groan. "Fine. Someone go get her and take her to my room. Leave her cuffed, I don't want her having total freedom."

CHAPTER 16
LEXI

Ice rushes down the steps towards me, and I try to keep a neutral expression. He's made no secret of the fact he hates me, but I refuse to show him fear. He grabs the cuffs and uses them to pull me to my feet. They cut into my skin. He slams me hard against the damp wall and shoves his face into mine. "I knew I was right about you," he spits.

"You should be happy. You were right, and Axel was wrong. I bet you're revelling in your moment."

He slaps me hard, and I hiss as the pain burns my cheek. His hand wraps around my throat and he squeezes hard enough so air is restricted but not so hard I can't gasp for breath. "If I was president, you'd be fucking dead right now."

"But . . . you're," I gasp, "not."

His fist connects with my stomach, and as I double over, he releases my neck. I inhale sharply and cough it out violently. "You better pray he doesn't leave your side," he whispers in my ear, "cos I'm gonna fuck you in every hole right before I slit your throat and watch you bleed to death."

I force myself to stand and look him in the eye. "Typical weak man," I whisper, smirking. "Threaten a woman with rape because that's all you have. Let me out of these cuffs and I'll fight you. Don't use your dick to hide behind."

He laughs, punching me again, this time hard enough to make me vomit on the ground. He steps back, sneering down at me. "I've never fucked a pig before. It's gonna be fun." He takes my cuffs and uses them to drag me up the steps and through a hatch in the ground rather than out in the open. It leads right into the main room of the clubhouse, where some of the men are hanging around. I get a few dirty looks as I'm led past, like a woman on death row.

The office door is open, and Axel and Grizz both look up as I pass. My heart twists painfully in my chest as they both go back to talking, like I don't exist.

Inside Axel's bedroom, Ice shoves me to the bed. "Pres looked busy," he comments, smirking. "Maybe I should take my prize now."

"I can imagine you won't be long," I say. "A minute, tops."

He grins. "Maybe I'll wait . . . until he's out on a run. Then we won't be interrupted," he threatens then leaves.

I take a few deep, calming breaths to steady my racing heart. *Fuck, now what?*

Duchess brings me dry bread and a small glass of water. She places it on the side, ignoring me. "Duchess," I begin.

She spins to face me, pointing a finger at me. "Don't you fucking dare try and make an excuse," she warns, and I press my lips together in a fine line. "I liked you, Lex. All the girls did, and we feel betrayed you lied to us. This is our home. Axel and the guys take care of us, and you're trying to ruin that. So, I don't want to hear your excuses. The sooner he gets rid of you, the better."

Her words hurt my already aching heart, but she's every right to be upset. So, when Cali comes in minutes later, I burst into tears. I can't take anymore.

She stays by the door with her arms crossed over her chest. "Why?" she asks.

"I'm so sorry," I say through my tears.

"He's a good man, despite what you lot think of him." It's the first time I've hated being put into the same category as the police.

"I love it here," I say. "I really do, and I messed everything up." I see her wavering as my breath catches in my throat because I'm choking on my tears. "I fell in love with him," I admit.

Axel appears behind Cali. He places his hands on her shoulders, and she glances back at him. "She's a trained liar," he tells her. "You can't listen to anything she says." He kisses her on the head. "Don't torture yourself. She's dead to you, to us all."

I sob as she walks away, leaving me alone with Axel, and for the first time since we met, I'm terrified. I don't know if he'll hurt me or what he plans on doing to me, but the real fear is of his rejection.

I watch as he moves around the room, gathering discarded clothes and dumping them in the basket by the door. "I don't want you speaking to the women," he tells me without looking up. "Even if you convince them with a sob story, it's not going to save you."

"Killing a police officer is a hefty sentence," I whisper, wiping my cheeks on my arm. "Life."

He sneers. "Maybe it'll be worth it."

He takes a seat on the bed, and I watch warily as he produces my mobile phone, all the while he avoids eye contact. "You need to call in, right?" I nod. "Keep it short. If you use any kind of code or you try some bullshit, I'll put a bullet in you right now." He reaches around his back and produces a gun, clicking off the safety. "And then I'll go after your dad. Tell them there were no drugs here. Put it on speaker."

I take the phone and press call on Jack's number. He picks up straight away. "What the fuck?" he yells.

"I don't know what happened," I say, my voice croaky from crying, though he doesn't seem to notice.

"Bullshit! They were tipped off."

"Nothing different happened, Jack. If they were tipped off, I would've noticed a hive of activity. Maybe you got it wrong." I make brief eye contact with Axel, desperate for him to hear it wasn't me who told Jack about the drugs.

"No," he snaps. "We had an informant, Lexi. They didn't get it wrong. We have pictures. It was there at the clubhouse, and ten minutes after I called you, it was gone."

"I should go. I'm in the club upstairs, and Axel's due any second."

"I want you out, Lexi. I'm talking to Commander Smithe and pulling you out. I warned you."

"No," I say quickly, "I'm not ready."

"You're done. You're no help to us, and you're getting too involved personally." He sighs heavily. "It's my fault. I knew you weren't ready."

"It's made me question my career," I mutter, and I feel Axel finally looking at me. I keep my eyes downcast because saying it out loud is way scarier than having it in my head. "My mum's here, and I, well, this club isn't all bad."

"Are you kidding me?" snaps Jack.

"I know you want to think they are, but they do good stuff too."

"Spare me this shit," he groans. "Look, let's meet to talk tomorrow. Don't make any rash decisions."

I disconnect, and Axel takes the phone back. "You're a

great actress," he says, getting off the bed. "You missed your vocation in life." He leaves, slamming the door behind him.

I wait half an hour before I decide to go to my own room. The door isn't locked, and I'm still handcuffed, but I need to shower and put some clothes on.

My room is exactly how I left it this morning, before my life turned upside down, and I smile at how different my day was a few hours ago. I use scissors to remove my bra, seeing as I can't slide it off my hands, then I shimmy from my knickers and get in the shower. It's a task in itself trying to wash with my hands bound, but I do the best I can. I wrap a towel around myself and go to the wardrobe. I'm limited on clothes that'll go over these cuffs, so I settle on a strapless top, which I step into and pull up. Luckily, I can afford to go braless. Then I put on some soft pyjama bottoms and climb into bed.

AXEL

I'm drunk and not thinking straight, which is exactly why Thalia is practically dry humping me as she pulls me along the hallway, trying to find an empty room. The club girls use the rooms on this floor, and most are occupied as the men don't take whores back to their own rooms. I don't think too much about the irony of that as Thalia kisses me.

I feel blindly behind me for the doorknob, and we fall into the room Lexi was using. I keep the light off, seeing Thalia might trigger sober me to kick into action and shut this down, because I know in the back of my mind, I'm doing it because I'm angry. The fact I'm in Lexi's room shows that.

I lean against the wall and close my eyes as Thalia opens my jeans and feels for my erection. It's semi-hard, but with encouragement, I'm sure it'll be raring to go. She drops to her knees, pulling my jeans down slightly and releasing my cock.

She licks away the precum. I shudder. *What the fuck am I doing?* As she sucks me into her mouth, I grab a handful of her hair and gently guide her to release me. "I can't," I mutter.

Thalia stands and presses herself against me. "You can, you're just stressed." She takes my hand in hers and pushes it under her skirt. I don't want to know why she's got no underwear on. "I've missed this," she whispers against my mouth. "Seeing you with her drove me crazy with jealousy." She grinds against my hand. She's wet and ready, so why the hell can't I just fuck her?

I pull my hand away, groaning. "I can't, T."

"Because of her?" she snaps angrily.

"I just can't. Maybe I've had too much to drink."

"Whatever." She pushes away from me and leaves, slamming the door behind her.

"Fuck," I mutter to myself as I fasten my jeans and go to the bathroom to wash my hands. I brace on the basin and stare at myself in the mirror. "Get your shit together," I hiss. "Pussy."

"I totally agree." Lexi's voice makes me jump, and I go back into the bedroom to find her sitting up in bed with the lamp beside her illuminating her face.

I frown. "What the fuck are you doing in here?"

"I was trying to sleep."

"You were meant to be in my room," I snap, angry she witnessed what just happened.

"Then you should've said that. I wanted to shower."

I arch a brow at how brazen she is to just carry on like nothing happened. "You've got fucking nerve," I hiss, ripping the sheets back. I stare at the bruises on her neck. "What the hell happened?"

"Nothing," she mutters.

I turn the main light on, and she blinks at the sudden brightness. The lamp didn't show how bad it was, and I feel a rage burn inside. There's a small bruise on her cheek, finger marks all round her neck, and her wrists have been bleeding. "Ice?" I ask because he's the only one who's been alone with her.

"You're not supposed to care, remember?" she whispers.

"To hell with that." I storm out the room, and I hear her call my name, but I'm too far gone. He's been trying to push me since the day I got back here. Now, he can deal with the consequences.

Downstairs, the brothers are playing poker. Grizz stands the second he sees me, and just as Ice turns to see what he's looking at, my fist connects with his cheek. He falls across the table, sending cards and drinks flying in all directions. The men move back, complaining, as I grab Ice by his shirt and pull him to stand. "I didn't give you permission to lay your fucking hands on her," I yell, hitting him in the face.

"You're lucky that's all I did," he sneers, spitting blood at my feet.

A growl leaves the back of my throat, and I lay into him until he falls to the floor. Then I stand over him, landing a few more punches. "Jesus, Axel," screeches Lexi. "Somebody stop him."

The men won't interfere, and Ice won't hit me back. Not without my permission. So, I pull him to his feet. He sways a little, and I smirk at how much the pussy's bled already. "Do it," I say, bracing myself. "You've been wanting to for so long."

He doesn't need to be asked twice and he punches me in the face. The prick doesn't even break my skin, and I begin to lay into him again. I hear Lexi making a fuss, and then she's pulling at my arm. I shrug her off aggressively, and she falls back, screaming when she hits the floor. I glance back just as Grizz pulls her to her feet. There's blood trickling down her cheek—she must've hit it on the table. Guilt replaces the anger, and I step away from Ice, trying to catch my breath. "Wait for me upstairs," I bark at her before heading outside.

Leaning against the wall, I light a cigarette just as Grizz joins me. I hand him my pack. "That was intense," he says, smirking. "You wanna talk?"

"No." I inhale the smoke and release it slowly. "I'm an idiot."

He laughs. "Ice deserved it. He's been asking for it since we came back."

"I mean Lexi," I mutter.

"She's hot. What man wouldn't fall for her?"

"Don't make excuses," I mutter. It only makes me feel worse.

"You're my President, Ax. I fucking respect you, but I'm serious. She came into the club with a background that had us not asking questions. That's on us all. She dangled her virginity in front of your face, brother—what's a man to do?"

I laugh, but it's cold and empty. "Tank wouldn't have fucked up like this."

"Are you shitting me? He made Ice his VP. That was a huge fuckup. But did the brothers question him? Tell him he was fucking it all up? No, of course, they didn't. Look, Axel, you're doing the job none of us want to do. You're allowed to fuck up. And it didn't do any harm. We got the shit out."

"But now, the police are watching us."

"They were watching us anyway. They wouldn't have her in here if they weren't. You gotta get your head straight, Pres. Talk to her. Find out what they know and what they're looking for. We can throw them off if we know the game."

I drop the cigarette butt to the ground and stare as the glow dims. "I really liked her, Grizz."

"You still do," he says.

"How the fuck am I gonna end her?"

"Pres, she's a copper. You can't."

"Then what do I do, just let her go? She wants to quit her job."

I feel him staring at me. "For you?"

I shrug. "Maybe she's saying that so I'll let her go."

"Or maybe she genuinely likes you too. She tipped us off, Ax. She could've sent us down, got a damn good promotion, and lived her life. Instead, she tipped you off. If they find out, she's looking at time. A corrupt police officer going down for aiding and abetting, interference with a case, or whatever the fuck they can get her on, would be the end of her. They'd eat her alive in prison."

"What are you saying?"

"I'm saying, do what you think is best. I'll back you one hundred percent. Just don't make any decisions until you've slept on it."

LEXI

I'm all out of tears. I sit by the window in my bedroom and stare out into the night.

The door opens and Axel fills it. I watch his reflection in the window as he moves closer. Seeing him lose control tonight reminded me of who I'm dealing with. It went against everything in me to stand by and watch him hurt another human, even if Ice deserved it. But most of all, it hurt me to see him hurting. He poured all his anger for me into that attack on Ice. I've done that to him.

"I gotta clean your head up."

"It's fine," I mutter.

He gently brushes my hair away so he can check the cut, but I flinch away, and he drops his hand to his side. "Let's go to my room. I've got a first aid kit."

"I told you, I'm fine," I snap.

"I don't know why you're so mad at me, you caused all this," he says, scooping me into his arms. "You and your damn lies."

He carries me from my room to his, dumping me on the bed. He reaches for the cuffs and produces the key, unlocking them. I immediately rub my wrists where they're bruised and cut from Ice dragging me.

Axel disappears into the bathroom and returns with the first aid kit. He lays it open on the bed and takes an antiseptic wipe. "Tell me why they put you in here."

"To spy," I admit as there's no point in lying anymore. "They knew you'd get into stuff to improve the club."

"So, this came about because of my release from prison?" I nod. "What have you told them?"

"Nothing."

I laugh. "Don't lie to me, Lex. I'm done with your lies."

"I'm not lying. At first, it was because you didn't let me in. Then, even when I worked shit out, it was too late."

"Too late?" he repeats.

I feel myself blushing. "I started to like you."

He scoffs and sets about wiping the cut on my head. "I really believed you did."

"I did. I do."

"Lex," he mutters on a sigh, "just stop."

He throws the wipe in the bin and takes some small Steri-Strips from the kit. "It's deep. I'll try these cos there ain't a chance in hell you're going to the hospital for stitches."

"There's someone feeding them information," I say. "Not me. Someone else. They had a tipoff you had drugs here and photographs."

"I know, I heard your handler. Was he even an ex?" I shake my head. "Christ, I'm an idiot."

"I didn't come here to rip your club apart," I admit. He finishes sticking the cut together and then takes my wrists and examines the dried blood. "I was offered a job here. I wanted to work in a big city, and I jumped at the chance, but it was just a lie to get me here. They pulled me into the office and convinced me to come here."

"What did they offer you, a nice promotion?"

"They used me cos of Widow. It was an easy excuse to get in here. They know you don't take in outsiders."

"Only I did," he mutters, wiping my wrists. "I fucking did and look what you turned out to be."

"I meant what I said," I whisper. "I'd leave the job for you."

He stands, putting distance between us. "You think I can ever be with you after all this? You're a copper, Lex. I fucking hate your kind. The thought of being with you, having sex," he visibly shudders, "*fuck*, that won't ever happen again."

It's early the next morning when Axel wakes me by pulling the sheets from me. After he cleaned me up last night, he slept on the chair, but looking at him now, he doesn't look like he slept at all.

"Get up," he orders. "Today, we're branding."

His tone is brisk, and it immediately puts me on edge. I slowly rise to my feet. "What's that mean?"

He grins, but it's not friendly—it's cruel. "I spent the night thinking of ways to make you hurt because Grizz won't let me end you. This is what I came up with."

I rub my hands over my face. "It's too early for this," I mutter.

"I made you my old lady, so we have to make it official."

"Just take it back," I say as he grabs my arm to lead me from the room.

"What better way to make you hurt than by leaving my mark on your skin?"

We go down the stairs and straight through the club to outside. I have nothing on my feet, so he lifts me, throwing me over his shoulder and heading around the back of the clubhouse. Once we're on the grass, he stops, and I smell fire. "There're two ways in which we cement our connection. I chose the old-fashioned way."

He dumps me on my feet, and I turn to see Grizz and Duke standing by the firepit. My eyes scan the scene before me, looking for danger, and when I spot the two branding irons glowing red in the flames, I gasp. "Surely, you're not going to . . ." I trail off while my brain catches up with what's happening. "This is a joke, right?"

He grins again, giving off manic vibes. I take a few steps back, and he grabs my hand, pulling me closer. "Tattoos can be removed."

"You can't brand me like a fucking animal," I spit, trying desperately to pull free.

He wrestles me until I'm in front of him, pressing my back to his front, and we stare at the fire. Anyone watching would maybe see this as a romantic scene, a loving couple watching the flickering flames. My palms sweat and my fight or flight sense is urging me to run. "Years ago, this is how they did it," he whispers in my ear.

"Until they realised there are better ways," I reason. "I won't have the tattoo removed. I promise."

"You say that now . . ."

"Please, Axel. Think about this. What you're doing is crazy. I mean, burning me, really?" He holds me against him tighter. "Please," I whisper, "don't do this."

"I've made up my mind."

"I'm no good with pain," I add, almost like an afterthought. "And—" Before I can finish, he shoves a rag in my mouth, holding his hand over it while Grizz pulls some silver tape out and rips a long piece off. I struggle harder, shaking my head from side to side as he secures it over my mouth.

"Be brave, officer," whispers Axel as he pulls my arms behind my back and walks me closer to Duke.

I stare wide-eyed as Duke takes the smallest iron from the firepit. He avoids my eyes as he moves closer. I feel the heat way before it touches me, and as he presses it against my chest, I scream into the gag until my throat hurts. The smell of burning flesh is overwhelming, and if I wasn't gagged, I'd probably have the urge to vomit. The pain is searing hot, and when he finally pulls it away, there's no relief. I go dizzy and white spots flash before my eyes, and then my legs give way, forcing Axel to lift me from the ground. He whispers words in my ear that I can't make sense of as my body sags. I pass out for a few seconds and only wake when the gag is ripped from my mouth.

"That's it, constable, stay with us," sneers Axel.

He places me on the ground and my legs almost collapse beneath me. I clutch the nearest log and ease myself onto the damp grass. Axel holds out a cold pack. "Press this against the burn. It'll soothe it."

I swat his hand away. In this moment, I hate him. I turn away slightly and vomit. It rips my throat apart because the only thing I have in my stomach right now is last night's dry bread.

Axel removes his shirt. I watch him from the corner of my eye as he tenses, turning his back to Grizz and fixing his eyes on me. Grizz takes the second branding iron and presses it to Axel's back. He grits his teeth, clenching his jaw but never breaking eye contact. When it's done, and the air is again filled with the scent of burnt flesh, he dismisses the men, thanking them. Neither bother to look at me as they pass.

"You're marked forever as mine," says Axel, grabbing his shirt from the ground. I don't answer him. I feel weak and sick, and my head is spinning. "Wherever you go, I'll always be with you." He smirks. "Every man you fuck after me will see my mark on your skin." He begins to walk away, laughing. "Show that to your fucking handler."

CHAPTER 17

AXEL

I stare out my bedroom window at Lexi, who is in the exact same spot I left her in by the firepit. She's staring hard into the flames, although she occasionally wipes her cheeks, which tells me she's crying. I shouldn't feel anything, but I do. I'm consumed with guilt. What I did to her was disgusting, and I fucking hate myself for it.

I spent the entire night watching her sleep, thinking of how much she hurt me and how she's made me look a fool, that when the idea popped into my head, I ran with it. And a part of me is screaming that she should be fucking grateful I haven't killed her, because if it was anyone else, they'd be ten feet under right now. But the other part is demanding I go to her and beg her to forgive me, so I can kiss those tears away.

Later, when I take her to meet Edward—or Jake or whatever the fuck his name is—I want him to see she's given herself to me. Maybe jealousy led me to it, but I get a sick satisfaction knowing he'll see it. And when she hands in her notice and quits the police force, I'll sleep a little better.

I eventually pull myself away from the window to call church.

The men seem quieter than usual as they file into the

room and take their seats. I stay standing, bracing my hands on the table. "Someone is giving the police information."

The men stir uncomfortably, looking around the room at one another. "Yeah, Lexi," says Ice, rolling his eyes.

"Not her... someone in this room."

There's more uncomfortable fidgeting. "I want everyone's phones," I add.

"No," snaps Ice. "No chance."

The other men take their phones and place them in the basket Grizz holds. "You hiding something?" I ask.

"No, but I need it."

"Until I've secured a place for those drugs, no one's contacting the outside world."

"You brought the spy in, and now, she's filled your head with shit."

"I heard the call myself," I snap. "I don't want to see what's on your phone, brother. Whatever messed-up shit you watch is up to you." Some of the men snigger. "But I can't risk anyone finding out what's going on right now."

"I don't know where the drugs are anyway," he snaps. "I was too busy tracking down information on little miss innocent out there. Something you should have done."

"If you've got nothing to hide, hand it over," says Grizz a little forcefully. Ice reluctantly places his mobile in the basket.

Once church is done, I hold Grizz back. "The police have photographs of those drugs in our lockup. It's somebody close. Lexi didn't go down there, so I know it wasn't her."

"I'll check Ice's phone first," he says with a smirk.

Lexi is still staring into the smouldering firepit when I go outside. As I get closer, I see she's crying silent tears. She's so lost in her thoughts, she doesn't see me until I sit down behind her on the log. My hand hovers over her shoulder, and I wince, pulling it away. Too much has happened.

"We got a meeting to get to," I say, and she jumps at my words. "Here's the letter you're handing over." I hold out the envelope containing the letter Grizz wrote for her to tell them she's quitting the force. She stares at it, not making a move to take it. "Let's go."

She pushes to stand, and I join her and offer a hand to steady herself, but she shoves it away. The burn on her skin is red and blistered. She didn't put the ice pack on it, so I imagine it's still burning like a bitch.

We head inside, and she goes straight for the stairs. I stop by the kitchen to get more ice then head up after her. She's looking through her wardrobe. "Keep that top on," I say, needing him to see her new mark. She shakes her head in annoyance and pulls out some jeans. "You need to put ice on it."

When she ignores me, I go up behind her and wrap an arm around her waist, holding her while I place the pack against her skin. She fights me at first but gives up the second the soothing ice cools her skin. "You hate me, I get it. Now, you know how I feel about you. So, let's put this behind us and move forward."

"And then what?" she asks in a low voice.

"I haven't decided."

"Jack will know something's off," she says.

"And you know what will happen if he gets a whiff of any of this. So, slap some makeup on, run a brush through your hair, and let's go do some more acting. You're really good at it."

LEXI

Jack is already outside my flat waiting. When he sees Axel, he frowns. I unlock the door, and they both follow me inside. "What happened to you?" he asks, sounding concerned.

"Nothing," I mutter then shrug. "One of the club girls, Axel's ex, got jealous. I'm fine."

"And that?" he asks, pointing to my newly branded skin.

I almost let out a sob, but Axel wraps an arm around me. "She's here to tell you she's done."

Jack's eyes fall to mine, and I know he's confused, wondering what's real and what's part of the act. "Axel and I are together. I can't see you again, Edward," I whisper. He relaxes slightly, thinking I'm still playing a role.

"Did he do that?" asks Jack, pointing to my neck.

"No," I snap. "I told you."

He peers closer at my burn and arches a brow. "Property of Axel?"

I want to vomit when he says the words out loud. "I love him." It's not a lie, and that fact hurts me more.

"So, stay the fuck away from her," snaps Axel.

We turn to leave, and I slide the letter Axel gave me towards Jack. It looks as though I've done it without Axel's knowledge, so he takes it quickly and stuffs it in the inside pocket of his jacket.

We walk back to the clubhouse in silence. Axel is a few steps in front of me, and I miss his hand in mine. It's stupid. After everything that's happened, I should be glad he's not interested. But I'm not. Not even a little.

Once we're back at the club, Axel orders me to work the bar. It's the last thing I feel like doing, but after everything that's happened in the last few hours, I have no fight in me.

The men hardly speak two words. There's no playing around or teasing. They order their drinks and leave to sit at the tables rather than at the bar. I don't know what I hate more—the fact I'm being excluded, or that they all know what and who I am.

When Thalia comes in, I want to scream. She smirks as she passes me and makes a beeline for Axel. She kisses him on the lips before seating herself on his lap. On his fucking lap! And I have no say because I deserve it. I almost felt glad last night when I heard him turn her down, but the way he absentmindedly twists her hair around his hand as he chats with some of his brothers burns my heart worse than the pain of the branding.

She sashays over to the bar and rests her manicured hands on it, making sure to fix me with a fake smile. "Ouch, that looks sore."

"What can I get you?" I ask.

"You know he hates you, right?"

"Gin and tonic?" I suggest as it's what she usually has.

"He branded you to remind you just how much."

I narrow my eyes and lean closer. "So, why did he brand himself?"

She grins like I've walked right into her trap, then she slowly turns to Axel. "Baby," she coos, and he glances over, "tell me again why you branded your skin with her initials?"

He looks torn, like he doesn't want to answer, but the pressure of the room all waiting to hear has him smirking, "It's a lesson to never let a bit of pussy cloud my mind again."

She faces me. "See, a lesson."

"We'll see," I mutter, pouring a gin and tonic and slamming it on the bar. "He loves me."

She laughs. "Please. He was blinded by your virgin pussy and your little miss innocent eyes. He'd never be with a copper—he hates them all."

"I'm a barmaid," I snap. "Just a barmaid." Because right now, it's the truth.

Her smile falters as she snatches her drink and goes back to Axel, sitting beside him this time.

Once everyone's gone off to do whatever bikers do in the evenings, I clean up and head for bed. Axel is sitting on the top step, staring at a mobile phone. He looks up as I go to move past him. "You're in my room," he mutters.

"I'd rather not," I say. Being around him and not being able to touch him is killing me.

"It's not a choice. You need to call your friend and explain the letter."

"I think it's self-explanatory."

"He's called you over ten times and left endless messages. He suspects I forced you to do this."

"You did," I snap.

He stands, pressing me against the wall, and I realise how easy it would be for him to push me right now. "My room . . . now."

I put the phone on speaker and call Jack. "Lexi," he says, sounding relieved, "I was worried when you didn't answer my calls."

"I was working."

"What the fuck's this bullshit letter?"

"It was very clear," I say, even though I have no idea what was in it.

"I can't give this in. They'll wanna meet you and ensure you're okay and not being forced into anything."

"I'm not."

"How the fuck do I know that when you turn up to a meet with him practically hanging off you? What's going on, Lexi?"

"I told you, I love him."

"What?" he yells. "I thought that was part of the act."

"It isn't." I feel uncomfortable having this conversation with Axel's eyes burning into me. "Coming back here was like coming home. I've never felt so a part of something."

"You're in love with a criminal."

"I haven't seen that side of him."

"You know he beat a man half to death because he spoke to his girlfriend."

"It's in the past."

"You're not talking sense. I need you to meet me alone, Lexi. I'm not accepting any of this until you do."

I look to Axel for guidance, and he nods once. "Okay," I say. "I'll text you when I can get away."

I disconnect and notice a missed call from my dad. "He'll be worried," I blurt out as Axel takes my phone. "Ice called him. He'll know I've been in touch with the club."

"I'll call him and explain."

"No," I cry. "Please."

"You lost the right to make demands, Lexi." I miss how he used to call me 'Mouse'. "I have something to deal with. You should sleep. You look exhausted."

"Thalia?" I blurt before I can stop myself. "Is that who you're going to deal with?"

He gives a cold laugh. "What if I am, Lexi? Maybe fucking her will make me forget I ever put my dick inside you."

"That didn't work out so well for you last night," I snap.

He moves fast, causing me to flinch when he pushes his angry face in mine. "I suggest you stop talking because I'm so fucking close to putting you in the lockup and leaving you there."

"When Jack's off my back, you can do just that. Do us both a favour."

AXEL

I made sure two of the girls would keep Ice busy for the next couple of hours so I could call church without him here. What I have to tell the men needs to be done without him making excuses, at least until we've decided what to do about it.

When everyone's settled, I attach the lead to Ice's phone and show his screen on the large monitor mounted on the wall so everyone can see the picture of the drugs he sent to a contact.

"No fucking way," snaps Duke, slamming his hand on the table.

"We think he did it to ruin me," I explain. "If I'm out the way, his life goes back to how it was."

"They would've come for us all," Duke says.

"But I'd have taken the flack, brother, you know that."

"The number traces back to a burner phone. Ice deleted the picture, but I managed to retrieve it," says Grizz. "He doesn't know we know."

"We know the feds use burner phones," Ink surmises. "It explains how they got to know."

I nod. "And how they didn't know we were moving them a second time. Ice wasn't around until it was too late."

"He was too busy trying to frame Lexi," says Grizz, and I frown. This wasn't part of the plan, but he continues. "Lexi has contacts, but she isn't a police officer. We did all the checks. She was seeing a copper, and he'd befriended her again when she moved here. She didn't tell him anything because she didn't know anything."

"So, how did she know they were raiding us?" asks Fletch.

Grizz glares at me, silently communicating for me to keep this up. "He warned her so she could get out. He didn't want her getting arrested," I lie.

"So, she isn't the spy. One of our own fucking brothers is," snaps Reaper.

"That's what the evidence suggests," I mutter.

"What are we gonna do with him?" asks Nyx.

"We're gonna treat him like we'd treat anyone that grasses on the club. We ride at three in the morning." I slam the gavel down and wait for the men to leave before turning on Grizz. "What the fuck was that?"

"Come on, Pres, don't pretend you don't fucking love the woman."

"We just lied to our brothers," I snap.

"It won't hurt them. She can't stay here if they think she's a copper. They'll never forgive her. Besides, she didn't tell the police anything, Ice did. He's the reason we were getting raided, and Lexi saved our arses. She risked it all because she clearly gives a shit about you. I bought you time, what you do with it is up to you."

"Her handler wants to meet her tomorrow, alone. He wants to check she hasn't been pushed into anything."

"Are you letting her go?"

"I don't have a choice. If she doesn't, he'll get suspicious. He already threatened to pull her out, and if they turn up here all armed and shit, they'll take her. Maybe it should be a test. Let her go and see if she comes back."

"That's a huge risk. What if she spills everything?"

I sigh, shrugging. "I have shit on her, right? She moved the drugs to Zen. She withheld information from them."

"I think she'll pass your little test. She wants you to forgive her," he says, heading for the door.

———

Lexi is still awake when I go into my bedroom. She glances up from a book as I move to my side of the bed and kick off my boots. "Nobody here knows you're a police officer," I mutter, keeping my back to her.

It's a minute before she replies, "I'm not. Not anymore."

"That's not how I see it and it's not how they'll see it. Grizz saved your arse." I pull myself to sit beside her.

She places the book in her lap. "Why would he do that?"

"Because someone else screwed us over. You weren't the reason for the raid."

She picks the book back up again. "I know I wasn't."

"But you still lied. I can't forgive that."

"I didn't ask you to."

"Arrange to meet him tomorrow," I say, turning out my bedside lamp. I feel her staring, so I look at her. "What?"

"What's the catch?"

"There isn't one."

"You're letting me walk out of here tomorrow to meet my handler, just like that?"

I nod. "How you deal with that will show me the truth." I turn over and close my eyes. It's a few hours until we ride out.

CHAPTER 18

AXEL

I bang on Ice's bedroom door and that of every other brother at exactly two-fifty a.m. "Meet downstairs," I yell as I move along the hallway. "Everyone up."

Grizz is waiting in the bar area. "I'll ride up ahead, get shit ready," he says, grabbing his bag and leaving.

When the men begin to gather downstairs, I whistle for them to quiet down and listen. "We're riding out in two minutes," I instruct.

"Where to?" Ice asks, fastening his jeans.

I head out the door without a word.

I'm the first to ride out the gates, with Duke, my Road Captain, to my left and Shadow, my Enforcer, to my right. We're missing Grizz, who'd usually be in Duke's place, but I don't feel superstitious about it. The other members follow behind, with the prospects, Shooter and Smoke, at the back.

It takes thirty minutes to get to the farmhouse my dad bought ten years ago. He had this stupid idea he'd retire here and live out his years in peace. He never got to carry out that dream. He never even got to sort the wreck of a building.

We dismount, and Ice rushes to me. "What are we doing here?" he snaps.

"What is your fucking problem?" asks Duke, stepping in front of me and squaring his shoulders. "All we've heard for weeks is your whiny bitch voice complaining."

Ice looks confused. "The last time we came here was to bury Matthews," he snaps. "I don't understand what we're all doing here, placing ourselves at the scene of a crime."

"We wanted to surprise you," I say as Grizz steps out the shadows. "We transferred this place into your name."

Ice frowns. "What?"

"Yeah, we thought it'd make a nice going away present," adds Nyx, laughing. Realisation dawns on Ice's face, and he begins to back away, shaking his head. A few of the men move closer together, making a wall that he can't pass.

"You don't look pleased," I point out.

"Why would I want a farm that's falling down and full of bodies?"

"Is it?" I ask innocently. "Oh, before I forget, here's your phone back." I hand it to him, and he snatches it.

"Did you know," says Grizz, standing beside me, "that when you delete pictures from your mobile, they're never truly gone?"

"I don't know what you're implying," mutters Ice.

"While I was inside, I did a tech course. I learnt how to retrieve deleted shit."

"Maybe try Lexi's phone," he sneers.

"I did," lies Gizz, "and yah know what I found?"

"That she's a dirty copper?"

Grizz shakes his head. "Nope. But do yah know what I found on your mobile?" Ice stays quiet. "A picture. A picture that said a thousand words."

"Like grass," I say, punching him so hard, he falls back against the wall of men.

"It's not how it looks," he cries. "I was forced into it."

"No wonder you didn't want to part with your phone," snaps Fletch, shoving him in the back so he falls closer to me.

"How the fuck is this fair? Lexi is a police officer spying on the club and she gets to walk around like nothing happened?"

"She isn't a copper," snaps Grizz. "You lied to cover your own arse."

His eyes widen in panic. "That's not true. I spoke to her dad. She's a fucking pig!" he yells.

"Enough," I snap. "Get him inside, face down."

He struggles when the men begin to drag him inside. I follow, watching as they force him to lie on the dinner table. Grizz rips the leather kutte from him before spitting in his face. "You don't deserve to wear this," he hisses.

I pull out my pocketknife and use it to slice Ice's shirt away. I stare at the club's logo on his back. We've all got the same tattoo, a skull with red eyes and a snake crawling through it. Grizz hands me the iron. "You're no longer a member of The Chaos Demons." I place the hot iron against his tattoo, and he screams out in pain as I burn it away. The men struggle to hold him as I move the iron over various parts until the ink's unrecognisable.

"My father trusted you to be his Vice President, and you screwed our club over."

"He was weak," he screams, thrashing around. "There was money to be made, and I made it."

I shrug. "For what? You're not going to enjoy it." I take my gun and place it against his head. He stills. "You had it good, Ice, and you fucked it all up for money. You should've given me a chance. I'm taking the club places, and soon, we're all gonna be rich."

He sniggers. "You don't have what it takes."

I pull the trigger, blowing half his head away. "Like fuck I don't," I mutter.

I throw my jeans and shirt into the fire and watch as the flames swallow them. I glance to where the men are loading Ice's body in the back of a truck. We can't bury him here now we've changed the property deed to his name. If the police ever discover the bodies here, they'll trace back to him. We leave his belongings in the farmhouse, just in case anyone comes looking.

I go to my saddlebag and pull out a fresh set of clothes, dressing quickly. Then we head out, most of us going back to the clubhouse, while the truck heads to the incinerator. We have a good deal going with the workers there, and it's the quickest way to get rid of a body.

By the time I get out the shower and crawl into bed, it's five a.m. Lexi is sound asleep, and I take some time to stare at her. It's my favourite thing to do when she's sleeping. The thought of not doing it anymore makes me feel shit I don't like.

I run a finger over the marks on her neck and then down to the area around my mark on her skin. I like seeing it there. She stirs slightly, her nipples hardening through the silk of her top, and my cock instantly reacts, straining to be near her. And I want to, everything inside me wants to, but I can't get it out my head that she betrayed me.

She groans lightly and stretches her arms above her head, which makes her top lift slightly, showing me her stomach. I trace a finger there and watch her skin prickle under my touch. I lean closer, running my nose over the softness of her skin and tracing light kisses there. She stirs again, this time running her fingers through my hair. I move kisses up her stomach, lifting her top as I do and exposing her breasts. I'm not thinking clearly as her scent hits my senses, and I take her nipple in my mouth. She squirms beneath me, sighing with pleasure as I slip my hand into her shorts to find her already wet. She grinds against my hand, moaning as I drag a sleepy orgasm from her. When she opens her eyes and smiles, I instantly pull away. Her smile fades.

"Sorry," I mutter. "I just . . ."

"It's fine," she whispers, pulling her top back down. "You're not ready."

"I branded you," I mutter, more to myself than her, but I feel her eyes on me. I place my head in my hands and groan. "I fucking burnt my brand onto your beautiful skin." I stand and stare down at her, shame washing over me. "You should hate me."

"Why did you?" she asks. "You gave me your reason when Thalia asked, but I need to hear it again, now we're alone."

I think over her question. "Jealousy," I mutter. "I want every fucking man who goes there after me to know I was first. You were mine first."

"And a tattoo wouldn't have done that?" Her voice is soft with sadness lacing through it, and the guilt makes me sick to my stomach. I sit back on the bed. Sliding the strap away from her burn, I gently kiss it.

"I didn't want you to be able to remove it. I'm sick, I know that. Fucked in the head."

"I wish I could turn it off," she whispers. "Then maybe I wouldn't feel this pain," she adds, placing her hand to her chest, over her heart. "I know what I did has hurt you, and I wish I could change it, but you need to know it was real, Axel. How I felt was real."

I tuck her hair behind her ear, and she lays her cheek against my palm. "I don't doubt it, Lexi, but I can't forget what you did. I wish it was that easy."

She smiles sadly. "I'd give everything up for you. I'd have your babies, even get married." She shrugs. "With you, I saw a future, and I never had that before." She gets onto her knees and wraps her arms around my neck. "I'm sorry I fucked it up."

My hands run up her thighs like they have a mind of their own. Gripping her arse, I stare into her eyes, willing her to make the first move. When she leans closer, bringing her lips to mine, I tug her to sit on my lap, easing my cock from my boxers. She rubs against me, kissing me like she's starving for me. I move her shorts to one side and pull her down onto my erection. I groan as I fill her tight pussy, burying my face into the crook of her neck and letting her adjust.

She holds onto my shoulders and lifts herself. I feel deeper, and each time she slides down my shaft, I hold her there, enjoying the feel as she squeezes me. She finds her rhythm and moves her hands behind her, placing them on my knees. It's the perfect position for me to take her nipple into my mouth again, and when I do, she moves faster, chasing her second release.

When she comes down, I take her by the waist and turn us, laying her on the bed. I lift one of her legs, pushing it to her chest, and I fuck her like I've wanted to since the day I first took her virginity. She cries out with each hard thrust, and when I feel her tighten around me for the third time, it sends me spiralling. I come hard, growling like a beast as I fill her.

I'm vaguely aware of the way she pushes against my chest, protesting because I've lost control again, which seems to happen a lot when I'm around her. But I refuse to move until I've emptied every last drop, then I pull from her, watching as my cum spills from her. I push my hand against her, making her jerk against me as I wipe the fluid over her inner thighs. It's animalistic, but I get a kick out of having her filled with me, smelling of me.

LEXI

He seems mesmerised, staring between my legs, occasionally rubbing and sending sparks flying each time. I'm exhausted, and I don't have the energy to demand an explanation as to why he's done this again, so I clamp my legs closed, bringing him from his thoughts. Then I turn onto my side, grabbing the sheet and covering myself. It's too early to get up.

After a minute, Axel shuffles closer. I'm surprised when he presses himself to my back, throwing his arm around my waist. It's seconds before his light snores fill the room.

I wake with a start. Axel has pushed me onto my front and is sitting over me, trying to push his erection into me. I bat him away, too tired for this right now, and honestly, I'm sore. But he persists, hurriedly groping at my breasts as he plunges into me. "Don't come inside me, Axel," I manage to grit out between thrusts that shove me farther up the bed.

"You don't get to decide that, Lexi. Not when you've screwed me over."

I frown, mad he's using that to do what he wants. And extra mad he still isn't calling me 'Mouse'. "Fine, but when I get pregnant, expect to be fully involved because I won't raise a child alone."

He grunts, stilling as he comes, and I wonder if the thought of getting me pregnant is what sent him over the edge so quickly. He climbs from me and goes into the bathroom. I hear the shower turn on and relax back into the pillows.

My emotions are all over the place. One minute, I hate him, and the next, I'm letting him fuck me without protection. I groan. It's like a never-ending, fucked-up mess.

"When you meet your pig, you need to tell him it was Ice who was responsible for the drugs. He was trying to set us up."

I inwardly scream. More bullshit. "What do you mean?"

"Ice," he repeats. "You're going to tell that dickhead that Ice was trying to set the club up along with Matthews. He's a known drug dealer, so it shouldn't be hard to fit the pair up for this."

I push to sit. "Now, you want me to lie and frame somebody else?"

The shower turns off and he comes into the bedroom dripping wet and completely naked. My eyes have a mind of their own as they run the length of his body, and I wonder how the fuck his cock is still semi-hard after so much sex. "Yes, Lexi, I want you to frame someone else, so the police stop watching us."

"You realise that won't happen, right? They'll watch you even more because they know Ice is a part of this club."

"Not anymore."

"What does that mean?"

"It means we de-patched him this morning. He's no longer part of The Chaos Demons."

"Can that happen?"

"It can when they turn into a grass. You make sure to tell him we didn't know about Ice's little side venture. He got the drugs brought in and some of the packages are at this address." He hands me a piece of paper with an address scribbled down. "He moved the rest with the help of Matthews."

"Okay, so where are they both now?" Axel smirks, and I groan. "Tell me they're alive." He shrugs, but I know by the cool expression on his face that they're very much dead. "How the fuck can I frame two men who aren't around?"

"You're a great liar, invent something." His tone is back to being cold and distant, something I hoped had passed since he spent the night inside me. Maybe doing this last thing will prove to him that I'm serious about us.

I roll my eyes, slamming the piece of paper on the side

table. "You realise I can't take the morning after pill, right? They won't give it to me so soon after the last one."

He pulls on some jeans and a T-shirt and shrugs. "Nature will decide."

"Decide what? If I have to become a single mum?"

He leans close, taking my chin in his fingers. "If I've put my baby in your belly, it's because I intend to and I'll help raise it. Nature will decide if we're going to get through this or not."

"Christ, Axel, why can't you just be normal? *You* get to decide if we get through this, not nature. Nature might force us into a position neither of us are ready for. You're not thinking straight."

He shoves my face from his grip and his eyes narrow angrily. "I haven't been thinking straight since the day you fucking turned up here and bewitched me with your virgin pussy. But you didn't mind it then, when I was blinded to the truth."

"You can keep punishing me, but it won't change what I did."

He pulls the door open. "Tell me about it," he mutters, slamming it behind him.

Minutes later, Cali comes in looking sheepish. I cover myself with the sheet and nod to let her know she can come in. "I am so sorry for how I behaved. Duke just told me you're not a police officer and you didn't lie to Axel." Guilt eats away as I smile weakly. "I am so sorry for being a bitch."

"Please, don't be at all. You were protecting your President. I don't blame you."

"I can't believe it was Ice all along. I know he was a dick, but a grass, really? I'm in shock."

I nod. "Me too."

"Are we friends?" she asks, sounding hopeful.

I smile, and she relaxes. "Of course."

Once she's left, I go back to my room to shower and dress for my meeting with Jack. I settle on a short summer dress, seeing as the sunshine has made an appearance, and slip on some sandals. I've always felt the need to dress professionally when meeting Jack, but this meeting is different.

I go downstairs, where a few of the brothers turn and watch me. Duke puts his fingers in his mouth and wolf whistles. "Looking good, mama," he shouts across the room. I blush as Axel comes out his office.

He frowns, taking in my attire. "What the fuck are you wearing?"

I glance down at the dress. "Don't you like it?"

He takes my hand and pulls me into the office, closing the door and the blinds. "Like it?" he repeats, scanning me. "I love the dress, Lex, that's the problem. Other men will love it too."

I smirk. "It's nice to be liked."

"You need to change."

His tone instantly annoys me. Who the fuck is he to order me to change? "No."

"What do you mean, no?" he demands. "Go and change the dress, Lexi."

"No. I like it."

"I can practically see your arse," he yells, spinning me around and tugging the back of the dress down to try and cover me some more.

I smile. I like that he's jealous, especially after days of indifference from him. "You remember I never dated Jack?"

"Did you shower?" he asks, inhaling into my neck.

I laugh, pulling away, knowing I ruined his plans to have me smelling of him. "Yes, but Jack won't know either way because it's not like that between us."

"Just change, Lex." He sighs. "Please."

"As much as I want to listen to you, I refuse to let a man tell me what to wear. Have a good day, Axel." I kiss him on the cheek and walk out the office with a spring in my step.

Jack is at the café where Axel arranged the meet. He's already seated by the window, and he almost looks relieved to see me alone.

"I ordered you a coffee," he says with a smile.

I take a seat. "Thanks."

"You managed to get away." I nod. "Good. Now, we can talk truths."

Truths? I want to laugh in his face. "Ice is your man."

He frowns. "I want to talk about you, Lexi, and how you're doing."

"Don't pretend to give a shit," I whisper, feeling tears in the corners of my eyes. I shut them down before they get a chance to wet my cheeks. I can't break now. "Look, I found out that Ice has been playing both sides. I know he's the informant."

Jack pales slightly. "Does the club know?"

I shake my head, and he relaxes. "But if I worked it out, they might. They discovered he was bringing the drugs in, and they've kicked him out the club."

"Impossible. He couldn't have done that without the club," he scoffs. "He's an idiot, for a start."

"I didn't say he was working alone. Nick Matthews, apparently, he's a big-time dealer?"

"He was reported missing over a fortnight ago."

"I think Ice got greedy. He used Matthews."

"Matthews was the one with the connections," he mutters, more to himself than to me.

"He told me everything, gloated. He thought he'd blown

my cover at the club. It was him who caused my injuries, and he told them who I was. I managed to convince Axel it was bullshit."

"Jesus, Lexi, why didn't you tell me? I'd have pulled you."

"Because I wanted to get this," I snap, sliding the paper to him. "It's the address of where Ice has been keeping things. He stores them there and shifts them on. I guess we made it easier for him, watching the club rather than him."

"Great work, Lex. That's amazing. More than we've had so far. What's the club's part in all this?"

I shake my head. "They don't have one. When they found out he was in on this deal with Matthews, they immediately kicked him out. That's why he's stopping at that address. Axel is trying to run the club right, plus Ice wasn't declaring the money he made from any of it."

He looks doubtful. "I know it's hard when you build connections—" he begins, but I cut him off.

"It's not like that, Jack. It's not been easy, but I did my job and got you the intel on those drugs." I pause before adding, "Did you know Axel saved me all those years ago? If he hadn't called my dad, I'd have ended up like my mum, or worse, dead."

"One good deed doesn't make him a good person."

"I know," I say, nodding. "And maybe he isn't. But I haven't seen the bad in him yet."

"He's the reason you want to quit everything you've worked for?"

"I can't have both," I state.

"If this information pays off, you could move up the ladder. That's huge."

"That's bullshit," I say, "and you know it. They're not going to move me any higher than undercover, and this isn't where I want to be. You haven't even married anyone because you've spent your life doing this. I don't want that."

He nods in understanding. "I get it, I do, but ending your career right before it's had a chance to take off is stupid. What happens if he loses interest? What if he dumps you?"

"I'm not just doing this to be with him." And I realise for the first time that this is the truth. "Doing this made me see everything differently. I joined up to make a difference, and I've been used."

"That's not true. This is giving back."

"It doesn't feel like it. I was dropped in the middle of a gang none of you really knew anything about. I was an inexperienced officer with little to no undercover training, and they used me because they were desperate. They didn't care what it meant for me to see my mum again after what she did, or how I'd feel to get rejected again, or how dangerous these men might be. So, Axel might get bored and he might dump me. But right now, I'm the happiest I've been, and I'd take a little of that over a lifetime of being a part of something that's a lie."

CHAPTER 19

AXEL

Each time the main door opens, I look up hoping it's her. Grizz takes pity on me and joins me, handing me a beer. "She'll come back."

It was a huge risk letting her go off like that. She could tell her handler anything and everything, which would mean the next people through that door are going to be the police. "I don't care either way," I lie. "I just don't want to go back inside, and if she spills all the information, that's where I'm going."

"She won't. I have faith."

"Glad you do," I mutter. "How the fuck am I supposed to trust her after everything?"

"Cos when she walks back through that door, with no career, ready to give her life up in Nottingham to stay here with you, you'll realise she's sorry. You can't punish her forever."

I take a pull on the beer. "I didn't expect to like her," I admit. "And it's a kick in the gut to know she lied to me. If she comes back today after framing Ice, I'll try to forgive her, but it's not gonna be easy, Grizz."

"Yah wanna know what I think, Pres? I think you're pissed

at yourself for letting her trick you. But yah know what, we all fuck up. Draw a line under it and move on. Learn from it."

I place my beer on the table and stand. "I can't sit around waiting. I gotta call her dad and explain."

"Good luck, brother."

I go into my office and close the door. Sitting at the desk, I pull out my dad's old address book. He's had this since as far back as I remember and it's got everyone's numbers, new and old.

I find Cooper's and dial it, holding my breath until he picks up. "Yep?"

"Cooper, it's Axel, President of The Chaos Demons."

"Axel," he repeats. "I go by the name Gary these days. I was sorry to hear about your father. I attended the funeral, but I stayed at the back. I didn't want to intrude."

"Thanks. That would've meant a lot. I never got day release to attend, but I hear it was a lovely service."

"It's been a while since I heard from anyone in the Manchester division. But I'm thinking it must be important if you came to me direct and didn't send someone from Nottingham."

"It's about Lexi."

"Lexi? Oh Jesus, tell me she isn't around that fucking witch."

"I don't know how much you know about Lexi's stay here."

"I know nothing, Axel. This is the first I've heard about it."

"Didn't you get a call from Ice?" I ask, confused.

"No. As far as I knew, Lexi was living in Manchester for work. I've spoken to her via text message, but she didn't mention you or Deborah once. Has she been around her?"

"Yes. She came here looking for Widow."

"Put her on the phone. I need to talk to my daughter."

"She's not here right now. Widow isn't interested in her—she's made that perfectly clear."

"Oh." He sounds relieved.

"But Lexi stuck around anyway. She stayed at the club and worked the bar."

"But . . . she's . . ."

"A police officer, I know." The line falls silent. "One of my men said he called you this week and you told him she was an officer."

"I can assure you he didn't. And even if he did call, I'm not stupid to tell anyone what she does, least of all the club."

"When Lexi gets back, I'll get her to call you."

"Why did you call? Is she in trouble with the club?"

"No."

"You're okay with her kind of work?"

"I'll ask her to call you."

"I'm asking you why you called, Axel. You're not making any sense."

I sigh. "She was undercover, trying to pin shit on the club."

"Shit. So, she is in danger?"

"The thing is, I fell in love with her, and well, then I found out the truth. But Lexi isn't in danger—"

"Because you fell in love with her," he says.

"Exactly."

"And now, you need my blessing."

"Actually, Cooper, it went beyond that. I already laid claim."

"You better be fucking lying, son. President or not, you ain't having her." The line goes dead, and I stare at the telephone for a few minutes before looking up to see Lexi watching me through the office window.

LEXI

"That looked serious," I say as I step into the office.

Axel places the telephone on the table. He looks relieved to see me. "How did it go?"

"Good, I think. I told him everything was Ice. He's sending a car to check out the house."

"Great."

"What will he find?" I ask.

"A well-planned setup," he says, rubbing his brow and looking stressed. "Now, let's discuss the dress."

I grin, doing a slow spin to show off the back. "It's a pretty dress."

"That should only ever be worn when your old man is by your side."

I arch a brow. "You're claiming the title now?"

"It was always mine."

"What happens next?" I ask, taking a seat opposite him.

He leans back in his chair and assesses me for a second. "I didn't expect you to come back," he admits. "I thought the cops would bust down that door and cart me back off to prison."

"It crossed my mind," I admit. "It would've been easier to set Ice up and still walk away. But I knew if I didn't try and make you forgive me, I'd regret it."

"You fucking hurt me, Mouse," he mutters. "Don't ever do that again."

My heart squeezes at his nickname for me. "I won't."

"I feel like a prick for doing that shit to your skin," he adds, pointing to my chest. "You didn't deserve that."

"You could've done a lot worse," I say, shrugging.

"You should know your dad is gonna come busting in here at some point today. He's not a happy man."

"You called him?" I ask, groaning. "Why didn't you let me deal with him?"

"Cos you wouldn't have told him straight."

"Oh Jesus, Ax, did you tell him you claimed me?" He nods. "I know how to handle him. I would've kept him calm. Now, he's gonna come in here and kick up a storm."

"He should," says Axel. "I deserve it."

I move to his side of the desk. "Can we call it even?"

He hooks a finger around my pinkie. "It's not as easy as just forgiving you, Mouse. I want to . . . fuck, I want to, but I don't trust you."

My heart sinks. "I came back," I whisper. "Doesn't that say something?"

He nods. "We just need to take it slow."

I nod in agreement, relieved it's not a no. "It's been a long few days. I'm gonna take a nap. Do you want to join me?" He shakes his head. "Well, you know where I'll be if you need anything."

Cali shakes me awake, and there's an urgency in her voice that has me sitting up. "What?"

"Your dad is here. It's not going well," she says, looking panicked.

I jump from the bed and rush downstairs, following the shouting to the main room, where Axel is holding his nose and Duke and Grizz are holding back my dad. I rush over, standing before him, and he instantly stops yelling at Axel.

"What are you doing here?" I ask, wrapping my arms around his neck and hugging him. The men keep hold of him, so he can't hug back but he kisses me on the head.

"Lexi, what are you doing here?"

Guilt overwhelms me and I burst into tears. The pressure of the lies and everything that's happened makes me lose control, and seeing his face is a reminder of my life when it was less complicated.

"I'm so sorry, Dad," I cry.

He shrugs Duke and Grizz off him and wraps me in his arms. "Baby girl, I told you not to come here."

"I can explain. Let's go for a walk." Axel stands, catching my eye, and I notice his nose is bleeding. "I want Axel to come too," I add, and Axel looks relieved. I need to show him I'm not hiding anything.

"That's not a good idea," Dad snaps.

"Please," I whisper, taking his hand and giving it a gentle squeeze. "I really love him, Dad."

He sighs, and I see in his face I've won this one, so I grab Axel's hand and offer a reassuring smile.

We head out and slowly walk the grounds of the club. "The police lied about the job," I begin. "When I got here, they asked me to go undercover, using Widow to get me in here."

"Bastards," Dad spits angrily.

"They made it sound so easy," I mutter. "I was already here, and I didn't want to come back to Nottingham, so I agreed."

"I should've come here too," he says.

"We set Mum up," I explain, and I feel Axel's eyes on me, but I have to tell the whole truth to make this right. "I let her see me take money from the bank and hide it under my pillow. I knew she'd come for it."

"She robbed you?" Dad asks angrily.

I nod. "She didn't admit it, but it was obvious. It gave me the way in I needed because I came here demanding to see her and that opened up my conversation with you," I say, turning to Axel. "I'm so sorry."

"I thought it was odd you'd be so stupid around an addict," he mutters.

"Then my handler elbowed me in the face, and I made out my attackers had been back," I admit. "I needed to be in the clubhouse full-time."

"Jesus," Axel mutters. I hate that I'm making him feel more like an idiot by telling him this. He drops my hand and folds his arms over his chest. The move hurts, but I stuff my hands in my pockets and continue.

"The thing is, being around you full-time became less of a chore. I sometimes forgot I was here to do a job."

"Did you give the police anything?" Dad asks.

I shake my head. "No, not really."

"Not really?" repeats Axel.

I wince. "I told them Matthews was in the basement."

"Oh shit," he groans, rubbing his hands over his tired face.

"They weren't interested," I rush to add.

"That's not the point, Lexi. They know he was here. You've put a dead man at my club. When they find him, they'll come here."

That anxious feeling returns. "I didn't mention your name," I mutter. "I told them Ice took me down there."

He relaxes slightly. "Okay, that might work. I can deny he was here, and you're the only witness who saw him with Ice."

"She ain't giving a statement if the police come looking," Dad snaps. "This is on you. She shouldn't have been let in here, not only because she was a stranger to the club, and you fucking failed as a president—"

"Dad," I gasp.

"But also because you promised me. You told me to get her far away from Widow and the club, and that's what I did. I gave up my life to protect her, and you just let her walk back in?" he continues to yell.

"I forced my way in here. Aren't you listening?" I snap.

"I fucked up," says Axel. "I did. But it's done. Just like her being a police officer."

Dad stops walking, and I groan, shaking my head in annoyance. Why couldn't he let me tell him? "It was my choice," I begin, but Dad's already got hold of Axel by the collar. "Dad," I scream, trying to pull them apart.

"You've undone everything I did for her," he accuses, shaking Axel.

"What were you thinking?" Axel shouts back, shoving him hard until Dad releases him. "Why would you send her to the police?"

"So she didn't end up here!" Dad yells.

"You forgot who you were," says Axel, more calmly this time. "You walked away and made her become everything we hate."

"Everything *you* hate," Dad corrects. "It's not my life anymore."

"Just stop!" I scream, and they each take a few steps back before looking at me. "I'm an adult. I make my own decisions. I decided to walk away from the police force, Dad. I've spent weeks thinking about why I ever wanted to join up, and it was for you. I did it all for you." I swipe a stray tear from my cheek. "You planted that seed, and I wanted to make you proud, so I went for it. But actually, being here made me see things differently, and isn't it time I started living life for myself?"

He looks taken aback. "I thought you were."

"I've spent so much of my adult life trying to be the opposite of everything she was because I was terrified I reminded you of her." A sob escapes, and I realise it's the first time I've said those words out loud. Dad made no secret of the fact he hated Mum. I got drunk once as a teenager. It was a friend's party, and I was underage. Her parents called Dad to come get me, and he was so angry. We argued, and he told me I reminded him of her when I was screaming the way I was. It hurt, really hurt, and maybe I didn't realise how much until right now.

"Lex, you're nothing like her," he says, rubbing a hand up and down my arm. "You're everything she wasn't."

"When you mentioned the police force, your eyes lit up, and I just wanted to make you happy."

"I'd have been happy whatever you chose."

"Well, I choose this." He sighs. "I choose Axel and the club."

"You've been here a few weeks under intense pressure. Come home with me, and we'll see how you feel in a few more weeks."

"No," says Axel, shaking his head. There's a glint in his eye that tells me he's willing to take a beating rather than let me leave.

"I don't need to come home to know how I feel. Don't you miss it, Dad?" I ask. "You gave this up for me. I've seen how these men are about the club—it's their life."

Dad looks around. "I did for a long time, but it was best for you, for us."

The gates slide open, and we all turn as Widow strides through. The second she spots us, her step falters. "Be nice," I whisper to Dad.

"You robbed off your own daughter," he yells.

"Really?" I hiss, nudging him.

He glances at me and rolls his eyes. "Nice to see you," he mutters.

She runs her hands over her hair, and I can't help but smile. She's still affected by him even after all these years. "I told her to call you," she says. "I knew you wouldn't be happy with her being here."

Dad smiles at me fondly. "She always was a stubborn one."

"How have you been?" she asks.

He laughs. "Really? After all these years, you're gonna act like we're friends?"

"Dad," I say, my tone warning, "please."

"Maybe we should leave them to talk," Axel suggests.

I nod in agreement, kissing Dad on the cheek and following Axel inside. He heads for the office, and I follow. When he spots me, he bites his lower lip, and I know he's trying to pick his words carefully, so I brace myself for a blow. "I just need a minute," he mutters.

"I wanted to be honest."

"I know, and you waited for your dad because that's when you felt safe to do it."

"That's not—"

He holds his hand up. "It's fine. I get it. I'm trying here, Lex."

"Mouse," I whisper.

His eyes soften. "Mouse," he repeats. "But I need time."

CHAPTER 20

AXEL

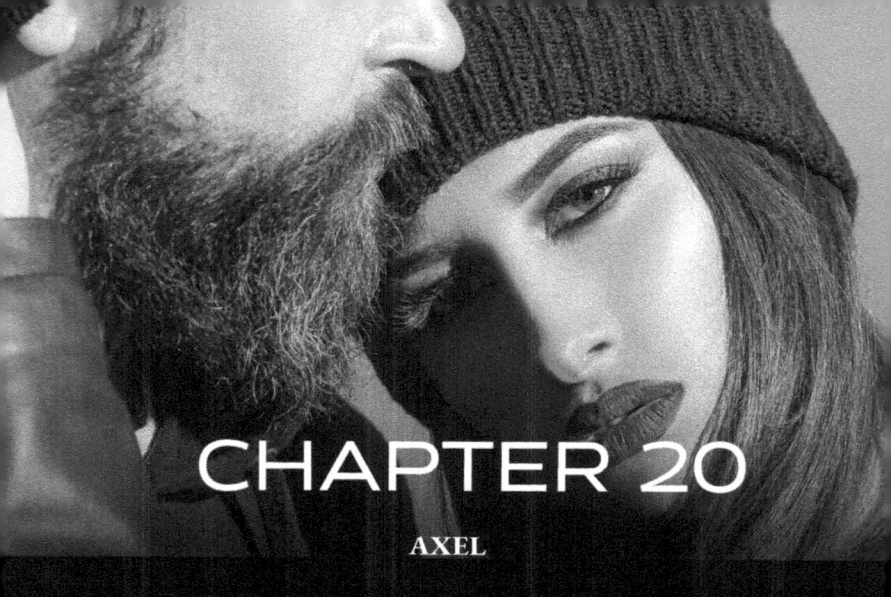

"What you got for us, Treasurer?" I ask Cash.

"Books are looking good all round, Pres. We've doubled turnover at Zen. All debts are paid at the bookies, and the new venture is giving us more money than we can manage to clean up through the businesses."

"Maybe we should invest in something new," Grizz suggests.

I nod. "That's the plan. All of you go away and have a think. We'll discuss ideas in church tomorrow." I slam the gavel on the table to indicate the end of business, and the men file out. All but Grizz.

"Cooper's sticking around?" he asks.

I nod. "For now." It's been two days since he turned up, and although things aren't as tense between us, he's still not on board with Lexi staying at the club. I've been through a million emotions thinking over the whole thing. One minute, I think it's for the best, but when I've tried to say the words out loud to her, they get stuck in my throat and I talk myself out of it. I've forced myself to stay away from her—being close clouds my head, and I can see I'm hurting her. She face. But I have to think clearly, so I don't fuck this up any more.

"And Lex, is she staying?"

I shrug. "She wants to."

"What do you want?"

I groan, letting my head fall back against the chair. "I don't know. The thought of her leaving kills me, but so does the thought of her staying."

"How can she make it right, Pres?"

"Man, she's doing everything she can to show me she's sorry. I hate watching her trying desperately to convince me because I don't think it makes a difference."

"You keep this up and she'll leave," he warns me. "You'll lose her."

"Why do you sound more worried than me?" I ask with a smirk.

"She's the best thing that happened to you, brother, and you know that. Fuck the bullshit that happened, it's done. Go make her happy."

"You make it sound so easy."

He stands, and I watch as he heads for the door. "It is. Do it or I'll march right out there and kiss her."

I laugh, but my smile fades when I realise he's being serious. I sit up straighter. "What are we, twelve?"

"Your choice," he says. "Are you gonna tell her she's staying?"

"I'm working shit out in my head," I snap, resenting the fact he's pushing this.

"Bullshit." He pulls the door open.

"Don't you dare," I warn. He grins, and I know he's going to do it as he marches off. "Damn it, Grizz," I yell.

LEXI

I look up at the sound of Axel yelling Grizz's name. "How's your day going, Lex?" Grizz asks, walking towards me with purpose.

I frown. "Good, Grizz. You?"

"Forgive me," he whispers, gently sliding his hands into my hair and resting his thumbs over my cheeks. "It's for his own good."

I open my mouth to speak right as he leans in to kiss me. His lips press against mine, and for a second, I'm shocked. Then his tongue sweeps into my mouth, and I inhale sharply as he kisses me. He pulls back, grinning. "Fuck, Lex, I can see why he was so blinded."

"You're a fucking prick," yells Axel as Grizz releases me, laughing.

"Relax, Pres. How did that feel?" Axel grabs him by the neck and forces him to lean back against the bar. "I guess it wasn't nice?" asks Grizz, laughing again.

"This ain't a game," Axel warns. "It's my life, and she's my old lady, and you just fucking kissed her."

Grizz shrugs, still looking amused. "I didn't see her pushing me away. Maybe if you send her away, me and her can —" Axel punches him hard, and I wince. "That's better," says Grizz, still grinning like an idiot. "That's the fire we wanna see. Cos she is your old lady, right? She belongs to you, and she ain't going nowhere."

Axel releases him and turns to me. His eyes are dark and his shoulders are hunched like he's got the world on them. His breathing looks laboured, and for a second, I think he might sweep me off my feet. But instead, he marches back off to his office, slamming the door hard.

I raise my eyebrows, waiting for Grizz to explain. He grabs a handful of ice from the bucket on the bar and holds it to his cheek. "Jesus, not like that," I mutter. "It'll burn your skin." I grab a clean cloth and hold it open for him to drop the ice into. "What was that about?"

He presses the cloth to his cheek. "He needed to feel," he mutters.

"Your cheek under his fist?" I ask, smirking.

"He loves you, Lexi. But his demons are telling him to walk away."

My heart stutters. "They are?"

"He needed to feel what it would be like to watch you in the arms of another guy, to realise he can't be without you."

"I had no idea he was struggling so bad. Dad told me to go home, and Axel insisted I stay. I just thought he needed some time."

"That's the last thing you should give him. That's when he talks himself out of shit."

I watch Axel in the office with his head in his hands and decide now's as good a time as any to lay myself out there. I take a deep breath and slowly walk over, knocking lightly on the door before pushing it open and leaning against the doorframe with my arms folded over my chest. He looks up but doesn't speak.

"I'm tired of creeping around you," I say quietly. "I'm so busy trying not to upset you that I'm losing sight of what I want."

He sighs, leaning back in his chair and watching me. "And what's that?"

"You. Just you. I miss how we were together before all this. I miss you calling me 'Mouse' and how you'd absentmindedly wrap my hair around your hand while you talk to your brothers. I miss you pinning me against walls so you can kiss me, or throwing me on the bed to . . ." I smile. "I miss us, Axel. You can trust me. Now everything's out in the open, I'll never lie to you again. Ask me anything and I'll be totally honest."

"Do you love me?"

I don't hesitate. "One hundred percent."

"Cos if we're doing this, we're doing it my way. We're in it forever."

I nod eagerly. "Forever."

"I don't wanna be that guy who checks your phone and—"

I pull my mobile from my back pocket and move towards him, placing it on the desk. "Have it. Check it. Keep it. Just tell me when my dad calls or he'll be pissed." He almost smiles. "I don't need the mobile. I just need you, and whatever it takes to make you trust me again, I'll do it."

He stands, moving around the desk towards me. "I wasn't distant because I was doubting my feelings, Mouse," he murmurs, taking my hands in his. "I'm asking you to change your entire life for me. That's huge."

Hope swells in my chest. "I wouldn't do it if I wasn't sure."

"You might wake up one day and regret it."

"Never."

"And I won't be able to let you go."

"Good."

He visibly relaxes. "I let your dad go out on my bike."

I almost laugh. Axel's bike is like his right leg. He never lets anyone near it. "That's huge."

"Right," he agrees, laughing. "And when he comes back here, I'm gonna ask him to take his kutte back."

I inhale sharply. "Because you saying that you wanna give it all up for me is too much. I can't have that when he's your life. We both need to be here for you."

"You thought you'd remind him what it's like to ride free?" I ask, smirking. "You're softening him up."

He grins. "Maybe."

"And then you'll be his President. That's weird."

He nods. "And he can't ever hit me again." I laugh, and he pulls me against his chest. "I love you, Mouse."

I inhale his musky scent and my heart dances with happiness. "I love you so much more. Is Grizz in trouble?"

He places his finger under my chin and tips my head back to look at him. "No. He was trying to help, but let's not tell him he's off the hook. You on the other hand," he kisses me gently, "didn't pull away."

"I was in shock," I argue, "and very confused."

"Umm, we'll talk about it later. When we're in the bedroom." He kisses me harder, pulling me against him until I wrap my arms around his neck. "No more kissing my brothers."

"Agreed."

"These lips, this arse," he squeezes my backside, "belong to me."

"There's no one I'd rather hear say that."

For the first time since I arrived in Manchester, I'm relaxed and happy. This is my home. It's where I was always supposed to be. Axel rescued me from hell and brought me back when the time was right. Because we were always supposed to be here together. We were meant to be.

THE END

Grizz - Book 2

Read chapter one of Grizz - The Chaos Demons MC...

GRIZZ

I scrub my calloused hands over my tired face and focus my eyes on Axel as he goes over last week's figures. "So, that about wraps it up," he says, running his fingers over the gavel. "Actually, one last thing." I inwardly groan. I've got shit loads to do today, and we've been in church an hour already. "Lex made a suggestion," he begins, and the brothers start to shift in their seats.

We all love the Pres's old lady, but she's been making way too many suggestions lately, from separating our recycling to holding bonding nights. "Just hear me out," he adds, sensing our protests before he's even spoken.

"Pres, no disrespect, but Lexi's last suggestion ended in Duke and Cash wearing face masks. Fucking face masks," says Smoke, and a few of us snigger.

"It was a damn pamper night," snaps Duke. "It's what we were meant to do."

Axel holds up his hands, and we fall silent again. "This is actually a good idea. Each of you will be assigned a club girl to watch over," he begins and groans erupt. "Look, Lex's got a point. It's a good way to keep an eye on everyone."

"What are we keeping an eye on the whores for?" asks Duke.

"Because they're people too," says Axel, shifting uncomfortably.

"Jesus, you need to get Lexi pregnant or find her a new fucking job," I mutter, standing. "We got better things to do than have pamper nights and watching the club whores."

Axel squares his shoulders. "Sit the fuck down, I haven't finished." I roll my eyes and flop back down in my chair. I might be pissed at his recent efforts to please Lexi, but I won't show him disrespect. "If we're watching them closely, they can't be sneaking off and giving information to our enemies, and fuck knows we got a lot of those lately. Not only that, but we don't know much about them, and if they're hanging around in our club, we should know everything."

"We know they're good at fucking and sucking, Pres. I ain't interested in much else," says Shadow.

"This club needs to feel more like a family," snaps Axel. "It don't feel like it did when I was growing up around here. So, you'll each be assigned to a woman and you'll do as I fucking say."

"And what exactly do we have to do?" I ask. "Because they're gonna think they're in line to becoming our old ladies the second we start showing an interest."

"We'll discuss it tomorrow in church," says Axel, slamming the gavel on the table to dismiss us. Before I can exit, he calls me back, and once everyone else has left, he sits back in his chair. "So, you wanna tell me what's going on?"

I tap my fingers impatiently on the large oak table. "Nothing."

"Now, I feel like you're trying to piss me off."

"I just don't get you," I snap. "You're the President, but every goddamn meeting ends with an idea from Lexi."

"Why's that a problem?" In truth, I don't know why it pisses me off, so I shrug. "You jealous?" he asks, smirking.

I sigh heavily. "I just don't want to sit with my brothers and put on a fucking face mask," I mutter. "I don't want to keep an eye on the whores."

He sits forward, looking me in the eye. "Brother, I'll be honest, I don't want to do that shit either, but when you get yourself an old lady—"

"I won't," I cut in.

He sighs before continuing. "When you get yourself an old lady, you'll realise you do whatever you can to make them happy."

"Well, I won't be wearing face masks," I mutter.

"I just need her to feel . . . welcome. She's trying to find her place in this club, and when there are hardly any old ladies here to keep her busy, it's my job."

"Make some brothers take an old lady then, keep her busy."

He grins. "Are you offering yourself up as tribute?"

"Am I fuck," I mutter, pushing to stand and heading for the door. "I've got shit to do. Don't bother me with anymore bullshit from Lexi," I say as I pull open the door to find Lexi waiting. She arches a brow. "Lexi," I mutter, nodding in greeting.

"I take it you told him?" she asks Axel, and I stop to listen.

Axel smirks. "Not yet."

"Now what?" I ask.

"It can wait until tomorrow. Go finish your bar."

———

The new bar is my pride and joy. It's a micro-pub with traditional furnishings and fittings I've restored myself. The club will use it to clean money, but out of all the businesses we have, it's my favourite. I've poured my heart and soul into it.

I place the last screw in the sign and climb down the ladder, stepping back to take it in. "The Bar," comes a voice from behind me. I turn, smiling at the sight of my neighbour, Danii. She runs the coffee shop next door to the bar, and while I've been working my arse off the last few weeks, she's been supplying me with coffee and bacon rolls. "It finally has a name," she adds.

"Perfect, right?"

She grins. "I guess so. I mean, we've been calling it that all along."

"Exactly."

"Coffee?" she asks. I give a nod and follow her into her shop. It's pink and girly inside, but as she explained when we first met, she wanted to make it hers, so she put her personality into it.

I take a seat and watch as she makes my coffee. If I was looking for the perfect woman for the back of my bike, she'd be it. She's gorgeous, with the body of a goddess. "Have you got a date for the opening yet?" she asks, turning and catching me looking at her backside. I sit back, and she smirks, placing the coffee down for me. "Cake?" she asks, lifting the lid on a fresh sponge. I give a nod cos she makes insanely good cake.

"A couple weeks, I reckon," I reply. "Almost done inside, and then I gotta have the pumps installed. My President needs to give the go-ahead and then I'm good to go."

"President," she repeats. "That's Axel, right?" I give a nod, and she returns a satisfied smile. "See, I'm getting good at remembering this stuff. Is he still loved up with . . . Lexi?" I nod again, and she fist pumps the air.

"A little too loved up if you ask me."

"Oh god, don't be one of those jealous best friends," she says, groaning dramatically.

I arch a brow. "I'm not jealous. I'm happy for him. Lexi is everything he needs, but she's got some crazy ideas and he jumps on them to impress her. Fuck, she had us listening to waterfalls and shit to try and relax."

Danii laughs. "Meditation?"

"Right, that's what she called it. You ever been in a room full of bikers listening to waterfalls?" I ask, and she shakes her head, still laughing. "It's not normal."

"I've never been in a room full of bikers full stop," she says. "I imagine it's a little intimidating."

"We're pussycats," I say with a wink. "Maybe you can come by one evening," I add, staring down at my coffee. "See for yourself." When I look up again, she's biting on her lower lip in that way she does when she's trying hard not to smile. "I mean, if you want."

"I'd like that. I'd like that a lot."

I take a bite of the cake, closing my eyes in appreciation. "Bring a cake. The guys will love you forever."

The following morning in church, Axel unfolds a piece of paper and clears his throat. "Okay, so yesterday, I told you about watching the club girls. Well, I've made up a list of who I'll be pairing you up with."

"Not this bullshit again," I mutter. "Pres, I don't have time to babysit, and what the fuck are we gonna do when they're working or with another brother? Are we meant to watch?"

Axel shrugs. "I don't know. I haven't thought about it." He begins reeling off his list, and when I don't hear my name right away, I know I'm in for some more bad news.

When he finally says my name, I groan, burying my head in my hands.

"Don't say it," I hiss. "Out of all the girls, you give me the hardest one?"

"Man, she's easy," says Cash. "She don't fucking talk. I'll swap her for London. That girl's got a mouth bigger than the city she was named after."

"No one's swapping," snaps Axel. "I thought long and hard, and Fable needs someone with patience." A few sniggers erupt and I glare at the men until they quiet down. "The rest of you fuckers get out," Axel demands. "Let me talk to my VP." Once they've gone, I fix him with an unimpressed glare. "The reason I paired you with Fable," he begins, "is because I suspect her the most."

"Of?"

"Talking to the police."

I frown. "You suspect the fucking mute is talking to the police?" We have our own inside man, and even though Lexi is no longer working undercover for the force, they're still getting information on us.

"She's a select mute, meaning she picks and chooses when she talks."

"And I can tell you now, she isn't gonna talk to me, Pres."

"I chose you because I know you'll get her talking, brother. Women can't resist that cheeky chappie shit you've got going on." He slides a piece of paper towards me. "These are the shifts she's putting in at Zen this week. Maybe walk her home or something, find out where she's been hiding."

"Great, thanks," I say, sarcasm dripping from my voice. "Is there any other reason you think she's the grass, other than she doesn't speak?"

"She hasn't been staying in her room at the clubhouse."

"So? The women aren't obligated to."

"Where else is she staying, though? She's too mysterious for my liking, Grizz. I'm trusting my gut on this one."

"If you're so certain it's her, why are all the other brothers paired up with a whore?"

"I can't single her out, she'd be suspicious," he says with a grin. "Now, go and do some fucking work."

LUNA

I gently lay Ivy in her Moses basket right as there's a loud banging on the door. I groan when she jumps, opening her eyes. "Fuck," I whisper before cringing. "Sorry," I add, picking her up. My daughter might only be a few weeks old, but I've vowed to stop the bad language.

I pull the door open, and my older brother, Nathaniel, pushes past me, followed by two of his meathead friends. My heart immediately slams faster in my chest. Since having Ivy, he's been easier on me, but I'm expecting it to return to normal any day now.

I follow them into the kitchen, holding Ivy close to my chest, and watch as Nate raids my fridge. "Got any beer?" he asks, piling meat and cheese into his hand.

"No, you know I don't keep that stuff in the flat," I say.

He opens the ham I was going to treat myself to later and eats it right from the pack. "Start buying it," he says between mouthfuls, "for when I come round." I give a nod, even though I have no intention of doing so. Stocking my fridge with beer and too much junk food will result in him calling around a lot more, despite him having a room at Mum's flat, which is just a floor above mine.

I hate his visits, but mostly, I hate him. He's just like my dad—a no good, waste of space who loves himself so much, he finds it impossible to think anyone could find him a repulsive piece of crap. And on top of that, he uses threats and violence to keep me and Mum in check. *He really is just like my dad.*

"You working later?" he asks.

"Yeah." There's no point lying. If he finds out, he'll make my life more of a living hell.

He slaps his mate on the back and gives him a grin, "See, told yah." He then looks in my direction again. "Danny here is gonna come over. See him right, would yah?"

"Clients have to book in," I say, shaking my head. "I can't just take walk-ins."

"Then book him in," he says, fixing me with a glare that tells me he'll lose his shit if I dare to push this. But since Thalia took over at The Zen Den, it's impossible for us to run our own client list.

"And all payments have to be made at the front desk," I add. "I can't do freebies anymore."

Nathaniel moves fast until he's in my face and I'm pressed against the wall. On pure instinct, I shield Ivy. "Then you better help him out now. Put the fucking brat down and get in the bedroom."

"Nate," I whisper, hating how my tone is pleading.

His mobile rings and he steps back, allowing me to breathe a sigh of relief. "What?" he barks into the handset. "On my way." He gives a nod to his friends and they file out. He gives me one last sneering look before following them.

I release a long, shaky breath and rush to lock the door. I really need to move out of this area to somewhere my family can't find me.

I've been off work for the last eight weeks. This is my first night back since having Ivy just two weeks ago, and although I know it's probably way too early to be having sex, Thalia has promised to give me an easy shift.

And so far, my evening has run smoothly, which is rare when you work in a brothel. *Trust me.*

By midnight, it's quieting down and I've just said goodnight to my fourth caller. I sit in the shared living room and relax back, praying my shift will end at one a.m. like it's supposed to. Thalia saunters over. "You heard what Axel's put in place?" she asks, filing her pointy nails. I shake my head. Since I found out I was pregnant at six months gone, I've spent less and less time at the clubhouse. "He's putting his guys on you ladies." I frown. "Apparently, it's all part of a new scheme that little miss perfect came up with. She wants the club to feel more like a 'family'," she says, rolling her eyes and using air quotes.

The bell rings out on the front desk and she rolls her eyes for a second time then goes to attend to the caller. A minute later, she appears with Mr. Green. I give her my best desperate look, but it's obvious I'm going to have to take the smelly fucker because there's no one else around. "Fable is free, Mr. Green," Thalia says sweetly, and I know she wants to gag because his bad body odour is already filling up the small space.

"Actually, she isn't," comes a voice from the reception area. A second later Grizz, the Vice President from The Chaos Demons, appears. "I booked her."

I give Thalia a smug smile and stand. "There's nothing in the books," she snaps. "How many times do I have to nag Axel to remind you bikers that you have to book a slot the same as everyone else?"

Grizz ignores her and grabs my hand, leading me up the stairs to my room. Once inside, I offer a smile, because in front of these guys, I never speak. A doctor diagnosed me as a selective mute when I was fourteen. I'd stopped speaking back in school after being horribly bullied. I was facing all kinds of trauma at home and having no break from it in school was the final straw.

I find it much easier to talk to people these days, especially once I know them, but I do it for the mystery with these guys. They like that I don't talk. It also makes me popular amongst the club, although I've only ever slept with Grizz once, when he came out of prison.

I remove my silk robe, letting it pool to the floor. Grizz shakes his head. "I came to take you home, sweetheart, not fuck. Get dressed." I frown, so he continues, "I'm your new babysitter. Pres wants us to watch you ladies." I shake my head. I don't need a babysitter, and I certainly don't need a biker poking around in my already messy life. I haven't even told anyone about Ivy. "I can't take you home at one when you finish your shift, so I'll pay for an hour and get you home early, how's that?" Weird that he wants to pay me but not have sex. I shrug, and he hands me a roll of cash. "Get dressed," he repeats, turning his back and looking out the window.

———

Grizz had no idea where I lived, so I had to write down my address. The rundown, three-story apartments were built back in the sixties and haven't had work done to them since. They're practically falling down, but since having Ivy, I've had no choice but to stay here instead of the club. I get off the bike and hand the helmet back to Grizz. He stores it away then removes his own. "I'll come up," he says, also getting off the bike.

"No," I say quickly, and his eyes widen at hearing my voice.

A smirk pulls at his lips. "Yes, Fable."

"It's just . . ." I hesitate, trying to think up a good enough excuse. "A mess."

He walks ahead of me, ignoring my comment. "You should talk more, Fable. You've got a sexy voice."

I sigh heavily and follow him. My ground floor flat might not look like much on the outside, but inside, I've made it beat expectations. So, when I unlock the door and catch the surprise on Grizz's face, I smile to myself but block the way so he can't get past me. Once he sees the babysitter, he'll ask questions, and that's the last thing I need. "I have to see the rest," he tells me, trying to take a step forward. I block his move again, and he frowns. "I'll leave right after, I swear."

The living room door opens and I inhale sharply as Jessica enters the hall with Ivy in her arms. "I tried to get her to sleep, Luna, but she's stubborn," she teases. When she sees my horrified expression, she hesitates. "Sorry, am I interrupting?" Before I can reply, she backs into the living room and closes the door.

I wince before deciding the best course of action is to ignore what just happened. I kick off my shoes and shrug from my jacket, avoiding his eyes.

"Who was that?" asks Grizz. The words clog my throat, so I say nothing, hoping he'll just leave. "Is that kid yours?" He shakes his head, complete confusion across his face. "Nah, you can't have a kid. It's tiny." When I still don't reply, he pushes past me and heads into the living room. I groan and follow.

Jessica looks up in alarm, almost wilting when she sees the large biker filling the doorway. "Whose kid is that?" he barks. Her eyes glance my way, and he shakes his head again, moving so I'm blocked from her line of sight. "Nah, don't look at her for answers. Is it her kid?" I don't see Jessica's response, but I can tell by the way Grizz freezes that she's told him the truth.

"What does she owe you?" he snaps, pulling out his wallet. I try and move past him, but he doesn't allow it. Instead, he stuffs some cash into Jessica's hand and tells her to get lost. I give her an apologetic smile as she passes, placing Ivy in my arms. She'll probably never come back again after this.

"Does the Pres know about this, Fable?" he demands, watching me as I lower my daughter carefully into the Moses basket. I shake my head.

"Luna," I say quietly. "My name is Luna."

Follow me...

I love to hear from my readers and if you'd like to get in touch,
you can find me here . . .
My Facebook Page
My Facebook Readers Group
Bookbub
Instagram
Goodreads
Amazon
I'm also on Tiktok

Also by Nicola Jane

The Kings Reapers MC

Riggs' Ruin

Capturing Cree

Wrapped in Chains

Saving Blu

Riggs' Saviour

Taming Blade

Misleading Lake

Surviving Storm

Ravens Place

Playing Vinn

The Perished Riders MC

Maverick

Scar

Grim

Ghost

Dice

Arthur

Albert

The Hammers MC (Splintered Hearts Series)

Cooper

Kain

Tanner

About the Author

Nicola Jane, a native of Nottinghamshire, England, has always harboured a deep passion for literature. From her formative years, she found solace and excitement within the pages of books, often allowing her imagination to roam freely. As a teenager, she would weave her own narratives through short stories, a practice that ignited her creative spirit.

After a hiatus, Nicola returned to writing as a means to liberate the stories swirling within her mind. It wasn't until approximately five years ago that she summoned the courage to share her work with the world. Since then, Nicola has dedicated herself tirelessly to crafting poignant, drama-infused romance tales. Her stories are imbued with a sense of realism, tackling challenging themes with a deft touch.

Outside of her literary pursuits, Nicola finds joy in the company of her husband and two teenage children. They share moments of laughter and bonding that enrich her life beyond the realm of words.

Nicola Jane has many books from motorcycle romance to mafia romance, all can be found on Amazon and in Kindle Unlimited.